ANDIE L. SMITH

Evernight Teen ®

www.evernightteen.com

ANDIE L. SMITH

DEDICATION

To all of us who have lost someone we loved, may we always recognize them in the world around us.

ANDIE L. SMITH

Andie L. Smith

Copyright © 2023

Prologue

My vision is blurry as I sit in the front pew of the church. The preacher is speaking, but I don't know what he's saying. All around me are voices. They pass through my mind so quickly, it's impossible to focus on the words being said. I recognize the tones, the emotion connected to the sounds filling my ears.

Sympathy. Confusion. Pity.

There's a tap on my shoulder. It's my mom, staring at me. Her watery eyes full of concern. *Why is she staring at me like that?*

Oh right, the preacher. He asked me a question. *What did he say?*

"Alex, are you going to read your poem?" my mom calls for my attention.

She stares down at my hands in my lap, at the paper gripped so tightly that the flimsy sheet is about to rip.

The poem, right. The one I had written for my dad. I'm supposed to read it. To stand up in front of everyone here and recite the words that I had put together over the last couple of weeks.

My mom squeezes my hand. The preacher is still staring at me.

I should probably respond, react, do *something*.

But I can't.

My feet don't move. My arms can't push my body up from the pew. My mouth doesn't open—my brain unable to form any words.

"Would you like me to read it for you?" my mom asks. Her voice is smooth, calm. It washes over me like silk, but it doesn't comfort me the way it used to.

I can't answer her.

She carefully takes the paper out of my hands, and my fingers react to losing the weight they held a moment ago. They shake uncontrollably.

The preacher backs up from the podium, my mom now taking his place. I hear the crinkle of the paper as she smooths it down on the stand in front of her.

I know the first word she's going to say before she even opens her mouth to recite it. But I can't hear it. I can't bear it.

Finally, the warmth returns to my feet. A small amount, enough to allow me to stand. Enough to allow me to run.

And that's what I do—I run out of the church so fast, I could have been a lightning bolt during a thunderstorm. My appearance brief, so sudden. And in the blink of an eye—gone.

The fresh air hits my face as if I've been slapped.

Where are you? I send the text before I can think better of it.

I wait. Two, five, ten minutes.

No response comes.

In defeat, I sit down. The concrete stairs of the church are cold on the bare skin of my legs.

A little girl is riding her bike on the road in front of the church. She's young, maybe four or five years old. A man follows her—her father, I assume.

The girl tries to turn too fast on the bike, her body toppling over onto the asphalt. Her father runs over to her, picks her up and touches her knee. She's bleeding. The screams of her cry are so loud they burn as they reach my ears.

I watch as the father carries the girl on his back, dragging the bicycle with them back down the road.

Before, I would have smiled at the interaction between the father and daughter in front of me. Now, I don't react. I don't feel anything.

I want to sleep. To close my eyes and never wake up. Or to wake up tomorrow and have all of this be a dream. To walk down the stairs and eat breakfast with my family. My dad sitting at the table laughing, pouring an unhealthy amount of syrup over his pancakes. Telling him I had a dream that something terrible happened.

That he died.

Him laughing at me, ruffling the top of my head like he always did, saying it was only a bad dream. But even those words wouldn't bring me comfort.

Because this isn't a bad dream.

This is a nightmare.

ANDIE L. SMITH

Chapter One

Death is funny. It's funny in a way that isn't really funny at all. The way you get a bad grade on a paper you worked so hard on, or the way you find out the milk you just poured in your cereal is sour at the first bite. It's funny, until it's not. Death is a lot like that.

It's been six months since Dad died. Six months for my family to mourn him, to grieve, move on. After six months, life should find its way back to some level of normalcy. Because life doesn't stop when someone dies. Theirs may have ended, but ours goes on. Or it's supposed to, at least.

Everyone else's life seemed to do that.

After the funeral, my mom went back to work. Can't have the one and only lawyer in the town take any more days off than what's necessary. My sister, Jenna, stayed at college, she didn't even bother to come to the funeral. Said her exams were more important. I don't know what test could be more important than burying your father.

They both bounced back easily, leaving me all alone, doing my best to not go utterly insane for the entire summer. I tried to keep myself busy. Between soccer practice and hanging out with my best friend, Blaze, I did everything I could to avoid being alone.

That's the worst part for me, being alone. When it's only me, my thoughts, an empty room. My mind unable to think about anything other than my own insecurities or my father's death. It hurts too much to think about him. How I will never see him again. He's gone.

No one else seemed bothered by that—him being gone. My mom said the funeral was the last thing we needed to do to be able to move on. For her, that was true. For me, it didn't make a difference.

Now that school has started, I'm thankful for a new distraction. Something to focus on each day, to keep my thoughts away from Dad. Thankfully, this year is different. I'm popular, and I owe that all to the most famous boy in school.

Jordan Tucker.

Jordan and I have been dating for three months, and I still can't believe it. I've had a crush on him for years—along with every other girl at Woodbridge—but I honestly thought I was being punked when he came up to me at the beginning of the school year.

I was at soccer tryouts about a month before school started. All the Fall sports got an early start to go through the tryout and initial practices phase each year. Since the school wasn't entirely open at the time, all sports had to share the same locker rooms by the football field, instead of the ones inside the gym.

Jordan was drinking water from the fountain on the side of the building while I waited to fill up my reusable bottle. I remember being annoyed because he was taking forever at the only functioning water fountain, until he turned around and I realized who he was.

"Sorry about that, I get a little thirsty from time to time." He winked at me and my knees went weak.

"T-that's okay," I stuttered.

Fiddling with the top of my water bottle to give my shaking hands something to do, I ended up dropping the lid to the ground. Jordan and I both bent down to reach for it at the same time, my fingers brushing the back of his hand. I reflexively pulled my hand away, trying to suppress the shiver that went down my back.

"I'm Jordan," he said to me, handing me the lid to my bottle.

"I-I know," I replied.

Everyone knew who Jordan Tucker was. He was a senior, and the school's star quarterback on the football team. It was rumored that he wasn't even going to attend the end of senior year because he was already being drafted to the NFL. His body showed it too. Although he was on the skinnier side, I could see the outline of his muscles through the sleeves of his shirt. His short dirty-blonde hair was spiked up at the front, and I wondered what kind of product he used to make it sit so perfectly. He was tall, a good foot taller than I was, and he smelled like a combination of sweat and aftershave.

He was absolutely gorgeous. And he was talking to *me*.

I felt self-conscious standing next to him, my frame only five feet tall, in a pair of athletic shorts and a thin tank top that hung loosely on my body, and definitely showed my light blue sports bra underneath.

I looked disgusting, and probably smelled that way too.

It was soccer tryouts after all, I was dressed like all the other girls running across the field behind me. My brown hair, normally wavy and hanging down over my shoulders, was tied up into a ponytail at the back of my head. I could not believe this was the moment I was coming face to face with my lifelong crush.

"You're Alexandra, right?" he asked me.

I was shocked that he knew my name.

A thought occurred to me then—this was an opportunity. To be someone different than the sad girl who never talked to anyone. Who ate her lunch in the bathroom stall. Someone besides the girl who came home to read a book before going to bed early on a Friday night.

It was my chance to be that girl I had only ever

watched in the movies, who goes from being incredibly lame to extremely popular overnight. I always thought it was impossible, but there I was, the opportunity practically landing in my lap. And I was not going to let the chance pass me by.

"It's Lex, actually," I told him, solidifying my new persona.

"Lex. Cool," he smiled at me, rolling the nickname off his tongue effortlessly.

His smile made my heart flutter. He had a dimple on each side of his cheeks, but they didn't quite line up at the same place.

That same weekend, Jordan called and asked me on a date. We went to the movies, and he held my hand the entire time. I wasn't even able to pay attention to the movie, too focused on keeping my heart from beating out of my chest and minimizing the amount of sweat coming from my palms.

He dropped me off at my house, and when he kissed me goodnight, I almost passed out in his arms. Jordan made me feel nervous and excited all at once. A way I've never felt before.

Being with him has been an entirely different kind of distraction. I'm constantly doing something, surrounded by people. Going to parties, football games, even sitting in class now is different. I'm never alone.

It's perfect. A way that I can move on, get past my dad's death. Like everyone else seemed to do so easily.

And what better way to get past it, than by going to my very first Homecoming dance.

Homecoming at Woodbridge High is one of the most exciting events of the year. Our small little town of Summersville, West Virginia, isn't known for much. Our population is insignificant, and we definitely don't have large theme parks like Disney World. But we do have one thing—a stellar football team. For the last two years, our team has come so close to winning the National Championship and we are determined to make it happen this year.

Go Warriors!

Being a junior in high school, I'm eligible to go to the homecoming dance without being an upperclassman's date. That isn't a problem for me this year, though. Not with Jordan being my *boyfriend*. My heart flutters at that word as I open my locker.

For years, every girl at Woodbridge wanted to be the girl on Jordan Tucker's arm. We all dreamed about what it would be like to hold his hand, to kiss him. To be the one he spends all his time with. The one who gets to wear his Letterman's jacket and paint his jersey number on her face for game day.

I have been that girl for the past two months.

I drop my books into my locker and laugh to myself, thinking about my first date with the most popular boy in school.

"Hey, babe." Jordan leans over my shoulder and kisses my cheek, as if my thoughts alone conjured him up.

My face flushes and I close my locker, turning around to face him. He instantly smiles and places an arm on either side of my body against the lockers, leaning in to kiss me.

"Yo, Tucker! Think fast!" We hear before the football slams into the lockers next to us. The loud *bang* the ball makes when it strikes the metal makes me jump.

Jordan rolls his eyes and winks at me, mouthing the word "later" as he turns around and jogs over to his friends.

"Sorry, Lex!" The group of boys yell in unison.

I laugh at them and make my way down the hall to my next class. My best friend, Blaze, comes up and loops her arm through mine before I can catch my breath, making some feminist comment about how boys should not be allowed to throw a football indoors.

I roll my eyes at her dramatically and take in her appearance for the day. Her ripped black jeans are rolled at the ankles, hitting the top of her combat boots. A red flannel flows over her shoulders and ties off at the waist, a lacy, black camisole visible underneath. Her fiery red hair—by which she got her nickname—is blown out and hangs low over her shoulders.

She's an emo goddess, and I'm proud to call her my best friend.

"It's like if I was a gymnast and wanted to do some cartwheels right here in the hallway, I would get detention because my sexy body would distract the other students," she rambles on.

"But you're not a gymnast," I tell her.

"That is so not the point!"

"So, you're saying the football guys are sexy then?" I ask her and raise an eyebrow.

We both laugh and she playfully pushes me out of her arm's grip.

"Hi, Lex!" A girl with glasses says to me as she walks in the other direction.

"Hey, Lex! I love your shoes!" Another girl standing by the water fountain with her friends calls to me.

My response is to smile and wave, making sure they know I heard them. I feel a little bad about not knowing their names, but I'm doing my best to be nice regardless. It was only a few months ago that I was one of them, a girl in the background waiting for her introduction to a whole other side of life.

"Doesn't that ever get old?" Blaze asks me.

"What?" I question her.

"All the smiling, all these people you've never seen before calling you by name. I don't know how you do it," she presses on.

I shake my head at her as we find our seats in English Lit.

"Lex, oh my gosh! Your hair looks so pretty today," a girl two rows over calls to me.

"Aw, thank you!" I say. "But I would die to have the natural highlights that you do." I smile as the girl turns back to her notebook.

My head turns back over to Blaze who is staring at me, mouth gaping and head shaking.

"What?" I shrug. It doesn't hurt to be nice to people who are being nice to you. I'm still new to this whole popularity thing, but I'm determined to do it the right way.

Blaze doesn't answer me, she pulls out her textbook and turns to the page Mrs. Simmons is referencing as she walks in to begin the lecture. Our English teacher is almost always late, and I never once saw her walk into the classroom without a Venti iced coffee from Starbucks in her hands.

I try to follow along with her lecture, but I keep looking back and forth between Blaze and the girl who commented on my hair. It's funny, really. Within a few months, I became the most popular girl in school. Sure, it's by association, but it's a change in my status all the same.

Blaze hates popularity and everything that comes with it. Thankfully, she continues to stick by me, and that's what matters most.

My best friend since kindergarten, Blaze and I bonded over having the same *Hannah Montana* lunchbox. Any girl that appreciated the best Disney Channel show ever made was a girl I could hang out with. We've been attached at the hip ever since.

When Blaze is mad at me, it's like a series of thunderstorms clouding over my bright day. The world is never spinning fully on its axis unless she and I are good.

I scribble a quick note on a torn piece of notebook paper and toss it over to her when Mrs. Simmons turns to the board.

Are we still on for tonight?

She opens the note and rolls her eyes at me, nodding her head and mouthing "duh" before giving me a small wink. Whether she likes the attention or not, one thing I know is that Blaze loves the parties.

And not that I would ever admit it to her, but I love being popular. There's something magical about not really having to try all that hard, and everyone adores you anyway. To walk down the halls and hear people comment on your outfit, your shoes, or your hair. It feels amazing.

Blaze doesn't get it, but I almost don't want her to. Most days, I want to keep this feeling all to myself.

Six months ago, I couldn't even see a reason to get out of bed in the morning. Now, I had more reasons than I can count. The boyfriend, popularity, making the soccer team. This could potentially be one of the best years of my life.

The ache in my chest is still here, but it's duller now. Less intense.

Glancing back up at the whiteboard where Mrs. Simmons has finished writing "Romeo & Juliet" I can't help but feel a pit in my stomach. Like the feeling I get whenever I leave for school, only to realize I forgot my homework and have to run back inside. I check my bag reflexively, seeing my notebook lying in wait. Even with my sigh of relief, the feeling doesn't disappear. It's still here, prodding and pushing against my gut.

Doing my best to ignore it, I start taking down my notes about R&J. The girls around me are giggling excitedly over the beautiful romance between the characters, and my breath catches in my throat.

I read the story when I was younger and thought the same thing, it was a beautiful romance that gave you butterflies and hope for love. But it wasn't until after my dad died that I realized how wrong I really was, how wrong the girls in my class are going to be.

Romeo and Juliet isn't a romance, it's a tragedy.

ANDIE L. SMITH

Chapter Two

I'm running. My breath quickens in my chest as I run down the hall, looking to hide anywhere, somewhere no one will find me.

Several people bump into me. Strangers. Vaguely familiar family members. Neighbors. They try to stop me, try to speak to me. I pay them no mind as I continue to shove my way past them.

I don't want to go in there. I can't.

Bam! *I smack into something and fall to my butt on the ground. It probably would've hurt, if I could feel anything at all.*

I look up at what I ran into and am surprised to see it isn't something, but someone. A boy, about my age. I don't know him.

"Are you okay?" he asks me and extends his hand to help me up.

"I-I'm fine, thanks," I stutter and ignore his hand, rising to my feet and smoothing down my dress.

My body finds a way around him. I don't have time to talk to boys I don't know.

The destination glows in front of me—the girls bathroom. I throw the door open and bend down to check each stall, making sure they're all empty. They are, so I go back and lock the door.

My chest is too tight, I can't breathe. Without hesitation, my fingers are fumbling around the back of my dress, moving the zipper down my body. Tossing it over a stall door, I feel exposed in my slip. The tightness in my chest is still there, removing the dress didn't solve my problem.

The sink. I turn on the sink and splash water onto my face. It doesn't work.

My legs weaken, I tremble to the porcelain floor and bring my knees to my chest. The floor is cold, it feels nice against my heated skin.

For the first time, I take in my surroundings. Looking for a way out of this mess. But there's nothing. Nothing in the world that can fix this.

My head rolls back onto the wall and I feel my eyes starting to close.

There is a knock at the door. A banging, so loud I can almost feel the vibrations from the sound. My name is called.

"Alex, open up." I recognize the voice. So tender, so loving.

My mother.

"I want to be alone!" I scream at her.

"Please, sweetie. Open the door," she says.

Without my permission, my body follows her orders. The door unlocks, and she enters the bathroom. Her hand goes to her mouth, shocked at the sight before her.

Good, *I think.* Maybe she will let me stay in here.

I make my way back over to the sink, propping myself up against the counter.

My mother follows. She takes a breath, extends an arm, and pulls me into her. I'm as stiff as a wooden board. My body doesn't soften at the embrace, but it can't break away from it either.

"I don't want to do this either, sweetie, but we have to," she says to me.

"Why?" I question her, surprised my lips were able to form a response.

"Because it's the only way we can finally move on. The last thing we need to do to get past all of this." She releases her hold on me, her hand waving around in the air as if she's swatting away a fly.

My head hurts, I don't understand what she means.

"After today," she squeezes my arms. "It will all be over. After today, we never have to think about this ever again."

I hear the clack of her heels against the floor before I register that she's walking toward the door.

"Come on, Alex," her voice instructs. "It's time to be done with this."

I wake with a start and sit upright in my bed, gasping for air. I only wanted to lay down for a quick nap after school, but I smack myself for not knowing better. My memories got the best of me. Again.

The bottle of water on my nightstand cannot be emptied fast enough down my burning throat. The ache begins to cease, and I take in my surroundings.

The purple paint of my walls, the rose-colored sheets in my hand. I'm in my bedroom, not back at the church. Still, the dream makes me uneasy as I go to shower and get ready for the party tonight.

My arms ache, like I can still feel the way my mom was holding me in the church bathroom. Telling me the funeral was the last thing we needed to do so we could move on from Dad dying.

Her words—"it's time to be done with this"—still fresh in my mind. As if my father's death could be chalked up to some to-do list, some unchecked item she couldn't wait to cross off.

Like a pile of clothes that no longer fit, ready to be taken to a secondhand store. An old sweater. Pair of jeans. The death of my father.

All the same to her—items to collect and discard, never to be thought of ever again.

****

The sound of police sirens blares throughout the

house. Tonight's party is at the McClean house. They're rich, and believe in huge, open-concept spaces that wealthy families drool over and high school kids love for any premature party-busting warnings with the way the sound carries.

From the echo I'm hearing now, the cops are probably about five minutes out. *Shit*.

"You'd think it would get old by now, right?" I stare at Paige as she says this and laugh. The other girls jump in with me and we all start to giggle together.

As if this is ever going to get old.

I've only known Paige and Becca for a few months, but they are already some of my favorite people on this planet. Well, for the most part. Becca and I get along fine, but Paige is another story. They're Jordan's friends and by default, they're now mine. Which meant they're now Blaze's, too.

It was the first week of school, and I had sat down at the lunch table with Jordan, immediately intimidated by the group of football stars and beauty queens sitting before me. No one seemed to notice me sitting there, and I thought it was weird that Jordan didn't introduce me.

"Hey, I'm Becca," said one of the girls sitting across from me.

Even sitting down, she looked shorter than me, which is saying something considering how small I am. She had on a plaid miniskirt, a light pink tank top, and a darker pink cardigan. Her short brown hair sat at her shoulders. If you glanced at her too quickly, you would think she was an anime character.

"This is Paige," Becca said, pointing to the girl next to her. I looked at Paige then, and instantly wished I hadn't.

She was absolutely gorgeous. My eyes glanced over her, noticing she had barely put any effort into her appearance. Her ripped skinny jeans sat over what I assumed was a white bodysuit, and a purple flannel was tied around her waist. Her long blonde hair cascaded down her shoulders and I couldn't find one single pimple on her face. She was beautiful without even trying. I wanted to hate her immediately.

"I'm Lex," I said to them.

"You're the girl whose dad died, right?" Paige asked me.

"I–uh," I stuttered, unsure of what to say.

The entire school knew about my dad, but I never thought anyone would confront me about it. At least not like that.

"Isn't your mom the town's lawyer or something? I'm sure your family got a huge payday with his will," she pressed again.

My stomach felt like it was in my throat. Her boldness stunned me and I wasn't able to move. No words came out of my mouth, none even formed in the back of my brain to push forward.

I nodded my head and stared down at the tray of food in front of me.

This was my first test for my new life, and I was failing. These girls would laugh me away from the table, Jordan would break things off, realizing how lame I really was, and I would be back to eating my lunch in the bathroom.

I was a fraud.

Paige looked me up and down for what felt like forever and I got the feeling she was deciding whether to physically remove me from the table or let me stay there so she could make fun of me some more. Her eyes found their way back to my face and she smiled a grin that didn't quite meet her eyes, so I assumed it would be the latter.

"So *you're* Jordan's new playmate, huh?" She looked at me. The way she emphasized "you're" made my skin crawl.

Becca choked on her sip of Diet Coke and slapped Paige's arm.

I instinctively looked over to Jordan for help, but he was deeply involved with some sort of football conversation with the rest of the guys. I was on my own.

"Um…" I tried to say but again could not find the words.

"She's his girlfriend, you mean," a familiar voice said behind me. Blaze pulled the empty chair out next to me and sat down, plopping her lunch tray on the table loudly. My sigh of relief could have been heard all the way across the school.

Paige and Becca winced from the sound of the chair legs screeching against the cafeteria's tiled floor. A smile grew on my face.

Blaze looked at me expectantly like she was waiting for me to acknowledge the statement that left her mouth. When I told her about Jordan, she was hesitant and kept telling me it was a mistake, that I was only going to get my heart broken. I told her even if I did, I would own it because it would be my decision.

That's what she wanted me to do now, own it.

"Yep, I'm his girlfriend." I popped the p on the word and smiled at the girls across from me. *Fake it till you make it, Alex.*

They looked briefly at each other once before both of their faces broke out into humongous grins and turned back to face me.

"There's a party this weekend. You guys should come," Paige said lightly as she stabbed a fork into her Greek salad.

Blaze and I shared a look ourselves. She winked.

A mischievous grin settled over her face. I guess I said the right thing. Maybe I wasn't a fraud after all.

We've been coming to parties with Paige and Becca every weekend since.

"It's the cops! Everybody get out!" The scream from one of the McClean twins brings me back to the present moment.

"Ready?" Blaze asks as she finishes slurping down her beer.

This is another reason why I love Blaze. No matter how bad of a situation we are in—aka the threat of going to jail for underage drinking right now—she didn't have a care in the world, as long as she finished the drink in her hand.

I laugh as she wipes the spilled beer from her mouth and nod to the girls. We all get up and leisurely head towards the door while we watch as everyone else starts to run and panic. Jordan always finds a way to get us out of these messes, so we never have anything to worry about. One of the perks of dating the quarterback, I guess.

"Oh, crap," Blaze says under her breath once we're outside.

I look up and see what she means. Left and right people are stumbling into cars and driving away. They are running all over the yard, the sirens only getting louder. It's absolute chaos.

And I don't see Jordan anywhere.

Paige and I share the same look of worry and start to search for anyone who has an empty backseat. She spots someone climbing into the driver's seat of an empty Hyundai Elantra, and my mind starts racing about how we can all fit.

Between Paige, Becca, Blaze, and myself, we could all squeeze into the back and Jordan could get in the front ... ugh! *Where is Jordan?*

My friends start to walk ahead of me to climb into the car, but my feet don't allow me to follow. I can't ditch Jordan.

"You guys go ahead, I need to find Jordan!" I yell to them.

"Are you sure?" Blaze asks me, concern spreading across her features. Paige and Becca are already in the backseat of the car, and the driver is starting to look anxious.

I nod to her. "We'll find another ride."

She climbs into the front seat and I watch them all ride off safely before heading back into the house, which is even more chaotic than the front yard. The LED lights strung along the walls are still blinking notoriously fast, and some idiot forgot to turn off the speaker so the house is still booming with electronic dance music.

"Jordan?" I call and weave my way through bodies, trying to get to the back of the house. *Maybe he's on the patio?* But if he was outside, he should've heard the sirens.

Finally, I reach the glass door at the back of the house. Sliding it open, I step out into the warm air of the night. A breath I didn't know I was holding releases from my chest. I call out for Jordan again but the patio is empty, only a pile of red solo cups catching my eye in the dark.

Shit. What the hell am I supposed to do now? Where is Jordan? The cops will be here any minute, and I'm going to be left with the wanna-be freshmen sobbing that their moms are going to kill them.

Panic builds low in my stomach. I have no idea what I'm going to do or how I'm going to get out of this. My eyes roam the patio for any possible solution. Cursing myself, I should've left with the girls.

"Are you looking for someone?" I look up to see a boy, who I think is my age, walking up the back stairs of the pool deck. I didn't even think there would be people by the dock that sits out there, and I feel relieved at possibly finding my boyfriend.

"Was Jordan with you out there?" I ask the boy.

"Who?"

"Jordan. Jordan Tucker." I stare at him, annoyed at his obtuseness.

"I don't know who that is, but no one was out there. Just me." He shrugs and starts to kick at the empty cups surrounding his feet.

I don't know what pisses me off more, the fact that he doesn't know who my boyfriend—the most popular guy at our school—is, or the fact that he doesn't seem at all bothered by the raid of cops that are about to be swarming into this house.

Maybe he doesn't go to our school? My head shakes at my own thoughts. *Not important. You need to get out of here.*

The battle inside my mind starts to grow. Not wanting to leave Jordan, but also knowing I cannot get caught at this party. The latter is worse. The latter wins. A decision forms before I can even second guess it.

"Did you drive here?" I ask the boy.

He nods his head and points to the side of the house, where I presume his car must be.

"Great, I need you to take me home." I decide quickly and start walking around the side of the house. Surprisingly, the guy follows.

The sight in front of me is so horrid I stop dead in my tracks. Debating whether or not to even continue or to run back to the patio and hope for the best with the cops.

It couldn't be an uglier car, if car is even the right word for it. A rusted, burgundy Honda Civic that looks way too worn down to be considered drivable sits on the grass before me. The passenger door appears to be a completely different color than the rest of the car, but it's too dark to tell for sure.

I glance from the car back to the boy, who is now waving his hands around impatiently. Thanks to the flood light on the side of the house, I can finally make out his features.

His shaggy dark hair sits perfectly over his eyebrows, and he shakes his head slightly to the right in a way that seems so natural and fitting for him, sweeping his hair over to one side of his face as he does so. His dark leather jacket cuts off at his waist to meet his jeans, which don't quite have holes at the knees, but even from here I can tell there are little shreds of fabric making them look slightly ripped.

"Are you getting in?" he asks me.

He's still staring at me, standing next to his old, beat-up car parked along the side of the house. The in three minutes more or less soon-to-be busted-by-the-cops house. Even from our distance, I can see how strong his jawline is as he's clenching it, waiting for me to give him an answer.

"Is this thing even safe?" I call out to him.

He laughs at me. "Does it matter?"

I raise an eyebrow and stare at him in disbelief. Something about his response makes me want to get in his car. Because if he doesn't care, then I shouldn't either. That, and the fact that cops will be here any minute.

My friends left. I have no idea where my boyfriend is. So, I do what any normal teenager under duress at a high school house party would do.

I get in a strange boy's car.

Chapter Three

The sirens are closer now and I mentally praise whatever beings above allowed this death trap of a vehicle to start and go fast enough to get away from the party.

"So, I take it the police interrupted your hookup plans?" He chuckles lightly and his eyes glance over my body, making my skin feel like it's on fire from his stare.

The outfit of choice I have on isn't anything bad, at least to me. My favorite bodysuit—a lavender purple color with ribbons tying off my shoulders, and a black leather skirt that stops about four inches above my knees. My feet are stuffed into a pair of old, white Converse. My wavy brown hair is having a good day, and it falls across my shoulders in a naturally wild way.

I thought I looked hot. Not skanky.

And who is this guy to judge? His outfit clearly screams *player*, but I'm not going to say anything about it. Not to his face, at least.

"What? No. I want to get home without getting caught." I self-consciously tug my skirt down a little further.

"Dammit," he spits out.

At first, I'm offended that his assumption of my outfit choice played some sort of role in the kind of girl I am. Like I said, *player*. But then as our entire dashboard lights up red and blue, I think differently. We. Are. Screwed.

I glance up and see the mix of colors in the rearview mirror. A knot forms in my throat and my body turns cold, sending my mind to another place entirely. Another night, where the contrast of sirens and LEDs through the living room window took my breath away.

The same breath I'm now holding so tightly, my chest begins to ache.

I can't go back there.

"Quick, lower the seat and act like you're sleeping," the boy interrupts my thoughts.

"I-I don't think—" I start to say, gasping for air.

"Just do it! And here. Take my jacket like it's a blanket." He throws his leather jacket onto my lap.

I don't understand, but my heart is racing too fast to ask questions, so I lower my seat and wear his jacket like a blanket. *Holy crap*, it smells good, like a tropical rainforest or something super earthy. The scent is a welcome distraction to my mind and my senses open up to it completely, feeling calmer with each inhale.

What is happening to me?

The officer gets out of his car after we pull over and starts walking up to the driver's side window. I really hope this guy knows what he's doing, or this isn't going to end well. The cops in Summersville are relentless for ruining our Friday nights. I can already hear the lecture I'm going to get when I'm dropped off in the back of a squad car. My lungs fill with air, holding my breath as the buzzing sound of the car window begins rolling down.

"Cam, I thought that was your car. You weren't coming from that party over on Tivan Street were ya?" I hear the officer ask.

My eyes remain closed, not wanting to glimpse the spinning hues of blues and reds again. I realize I didn't even know my driver's name until the officer said it so casually. Cam.

His name rolls around in the back of my mind, but comes up blank. My earlier thoughts of this boy are confirmed, I don't know him. The officer does, which isn't a surprise. For the most part, Summersville is a small town, and everyone kind of knows everyone around here. Except for me, it seems.

Chill out, it's nothing more than his name. It doesn't matter anyways. Instinctively, my eyes roll at my thoughts but they are still closed, which ends up making me feel nauseated and ready to throw up that last beer I had.

"No, sir, Officer Hunter. I'm offended you think I would attend something as juvenile and trashy as that," he says.

Oh, okay, so I'm juvenile and trashy. Noted, *Cam.*

My eyelids flutter and my breath is light, inhaling the rainforest but exhaling slowly, so the smell of alcohol doesn't become too strong in such a small space.

"I was on a date," he adds.

Excuse me? My teeth find my bottom lip in reaction—too hard. I flinch at the sudden blast of pain. The sour taste of blood hits my tongue and a wave of nausea hits me again. I don't even know this guy, but I am going to kill him when we get out of this.

If we get out of this.

"On a date, huh? With this lady over there? Is she okay? She's not drunk, is she?" The cop—Officer Hunter apparently—asks with a laugh.

"No, sir, she fell asleep during the drive-in movie we were at over in the town square. Apparently, romantic comedies aren't her thing. Who knew!" Cam's voice fluctuates a little at the words, and I grimace at how bad of a liar he is.

Say less words, I mentally tell him.

"I decided not to bore her, or myself any longer and take her home," Cam replies.

Okay, I think. Maybe he is going to get us out of this.

Though I don't know if anyone would believe that

Alexandra Marsh went to a drive-in movie with a random guy instead of being at a party with her famous football boyfriend.

"Well, I'm glad to hear you weren't involved in that party scandal. Kids these days don't know when to stop before they ruin their lives. Y'all have a good night, and drive safe." The cop chuckles as he walks back to his car.

"You, too, Officer Hunter! Say hello to little Brittany for me!" Cam yells out the window.

I stay down until I see the officer's car pull in front of us and drive a good distance away. Despite knowing better, my eyes lift and I watch the bright LEDs disappear down the road. The knot is back in my throat, my mind trying so hard to go back to that night.

"Okay, you're clear," I hear Cam say, but I can't answer him. The seatbelt is suddenly too tight around my chest, as if it's wrapped around my windpipe instead.

"Hey, you okay?" The boy, Cam, asks me again.

The jacket is still on my lap. My fingers clutch to it, not ready to let go of its earthy aroma yet. Cam doesn't reach over to take it back either.

"I-I," is all I can make out. My breath is rising faster, dark spots beginning to cloud my vision. *This cannot be happening right now.*

The passenger door opens and Cam's voice is filtering in from further away than it was a moment ago. *When did he leave his seat?*

"Hey, it's okay. I'm going to lean over and undo your seatbelt, okay?" His voice sounds gurgled now, like it's underwater. I try to nod my head, unable to form any words.

He does what he said, leaning over me, a soft scent of pine and amber filling my nose before I hear the soft click of the seatbelt unbuckling. My chest feels lighter almost immediately, but my breaths are still coming in and out quickly.

"What–what's happening?" I ask him, to myself, to anyone who can hear me.

"Shh, it's gonna be fine. I'm going to help you out of the car, okay? We're just going to sit down on the ground for a minute."

Warm hands find mine and before I know it, a cold surface is under my legs. I press my palms down into the concrete and glance up for the first time since the dark clouds over my eyes began to fade. The road. We're sitting on the side of the road.

Cam comes into view now, his brows pulled together as he crouches down beside me. "I want you to try something for me, okay? Close your eyes and take a deep breath, and when you exhale, open them and find something to focus on as you breathe again."

My body listens to him before I can ask any questions. I close my eyes and inhale so deeply, I pull at muscles all the way down in my toes. When I breathe out, my eyes open and focus on the first thing I can see—him. It's pitch black out here, but I stare at the dark tendrils of his hair curling over his eyebrows, still lowered together in concern. A stray lock of hair is going the other direction as the rest, and I wonder for a moment if he gets frustrated over trying to fix it throughout the day.

In my distracted thoughts, I feel my breathing return to normal. My vision is clear, and I almost forget what led me to sitting down on the side of the road in the first place.

"What happened?"

"I think you were having a panic attack. Has that happened before?" he asks me.

The way my vision darkened and my breathing hastened felt so familiar, like déjà vu—something that may have happened to me before—but the memory is so foggy I'm not quite sure.

"I don't know," I say honestly.

"My little brother gets them a lot." Cam pushes himself off his knees and rises to his feet. He extends one hand, offering to help me up. I take it.

"Is that how you knew what to do? To fix it?"

Cam scrunches his mouth in response to my question, and I wonder if there's something wrong with what I asked. "I wouldn't say I know how to fix it, I think panic attacks are different for everyone. But my mom taught us that breathing trick, and yes, it usually helps my brother calm down."

He leads me back over to the passenger side of the car, his hand hovering gently over my back. I climb into the seat, picking up the jacket from where it fell on the floor and holding it back out to its owner. He takes it from me, his fingers brushing against mine and sending a shock down my arm.

"Are you ready to go home?" he asks once he's back in the driver's seat.

I nod. "I live on WestMin Drive. Do you know how to get there from here?" I hope he does. After what just happened, all I want to do is shower and go to bed. Plus, I'm still nervous about where Jordan might have ended up.

Cam looks at me and one side of his mouth lifts up in a small smile. *Wait a minute. I know that look.* He's looking at me with pity. Sympathy. It's the same look I received from strangers, neighbors, my friends when my dad died. I really hate that look.

Anger fuels in my stomach, and I do my best to push it down. The sudden flush in my face gives me away.

"Yeah, I do. I'm Cameron by the way," his tone is

casual, as if he isn't at all affected by what happened a moment ago. And by what happened, I mean my complete and total freakout on the side of the road.

My breath hitches, and I realize he could tell anyone about what occurred tonight. Word would spread fast, and soon Jordan—not to mention the entire school—would think I'm a lunatic.

I don't know this boy. He doesn't know me. *Should I tell him my name?*

My mind pushes me to thank him for saving my ass tonight. And for what he did after. It's the least I could do.

Does he even go to my school? If he doesn't, this will make tonight's events much easier to digest. Much easier to avoid. And my name won't even matter.

My lips make the decision before my brain can even catch up to the question.

"I'm Alex. And thank you… for the ride." *And the other thing.*

****

I linger on the porch for a moment longer than normal as I watch Cameron drive away. A pit forms in my stomach, but vanishes almost as soon as it appears. *You're not going to see him again.* He won't tell anyone. Especially not Jordan.

I laugh at myself, arguing with my inner thoughts. Trying to find any reason I can to avoid going into the big, wooden, yellow house in front of me.

My mom is a lawyer, the town's only one, to be exact, but you wouldn't know it by looking at our house. We live in a pretty normal neighborhood that isn't even gated. Then again, it's Summersville. Nothing bad ever happens here.

For the most part.

We live on WestMin Drive, deep in the heart of

the Summersville suburbs. Our house is old, but from all the work my mom has done on it, you would think it was built last year.

Yellow wood panels cover the second story of the house, and the bottom half is a gorgeous gray and black brick layover that sits on the foundation. It has small radius-shaped windows, the kind that you would see in a medieval church building.

The front lawn is average-sized, but my mom's garden by the front door is what she's most proud of. She grows anything from lima beans to sunflowers, and never pays anyone to take care of it for her, despite how busy she is.

When I was little, she would let me help her plant new crops and harvest what was ready. As I grew up, I got busy with soccer and school and didn't have time to play garden with her anymore. I told her to hire somebody to come out and do it for her.

"Never pay anyone to take care of something so dear to your heart, they won't do it right," she would tell me.

I stare at the dark blue door before me now and for the second time this evening, am taken back to that night.

That horrible night that changed my life forever.

I had gotten home from my soccer game, deciding to ride with one of my friends on the team to grab pizza after instead of the usual drive home with my dad.

My mom was crying in the kitchen.

Noticing me, she brought me over to the living room and sat me down in what used to be my favorite chair. An oversized blue recliner that always squished a little too much when you sat in it.

"Alex, baby, I have something to tell you," my mom said to me.

She was rubbing the side of my face with her hand. It was weird, and for a moment, I was scared that I was in trouble.

"Sweetie," she choked out through broken sobs. "Your father was in an accident. He—" she briefly wiped at her eyes before grabbing my hand again. "He's gone."

Reflexively, I looked around the room. Waiting for my dad to join the conversation.

"What do you mean gone?" I asked.

She didn't answer me, only covered her mouth with the palm of her hand.

"He's not coming home?" I didn't understand. *Where was my dad?*

"No, he's not coming home, baby. He didn't survive the accident. He's–he's dead," she said the words so quickly that I almost didn't hear her.

My heart had stopped beating.

The insides of my stomach plummeted to the floor. It felt like being on a drop ride at an amusement park, only the part where you fall to the ground never ended. But it wasn't exciting. It wasn't fun.

It was terrifying.

Those dreaded words—*he's dead*—rang in my ears.

My mom continued to talk, but I had no idea what she was saying. My breath sped up faster than my brain could. The room started to spin, a deep black began to cloud over my vision. Sweat dripped down my forehead, into my eyes. It burned.

"Alex?" my mom's voice rang out in the darkness.

The air changed. A cool breeze whipped over my skin. My lungs burned for oxygen, aching to breathe. I was swimming, drowning, reaching for the surface, but plummeting back underneath the water.

My body shook. I was hoping someone was waking me up from the nightmare.

"Alex, look at me!" It was my sister's voice that time.

Slowly, I started to swim up. The hold against my legs in the deep end released me. The black dots went away. My vision came back into focus. My mother and my sister were kneeling in front of me, concerned faces looking over every inch of my body.

Something was forced into my hand. A glass of water. I drank the whole thing in a matter of seconds.

A string of red and blue lights shined through the windows of the house and pulled my mom's attention away from me. Jenna pushed me to one side of the chair, her body resting next to mine a moment after.

My mom was at the door, speaking to someone. She shut the door, but her hands were no longer empty. A plastic bag sat between them, holding a pair of car keys, a wallet, and a phone. Jenna gasped. I realized what the objects were.

My *dad's* car keys, wallet, and phone.

A wave of confusion washed over me. *How could the entirety of someone's life fit into one tiny Ziploc bag?*

My mom set the bag on the counter, but the contents were still visible to me. I noticed a small piece of orange and white paper sticking out of the wallet. The cops probably didn't even look at it. My mom ignored it… a random receipt from wherever my dad had been that day.

But I recognized it immediately.

The logo on the receipt stood out like a rainbow of color in a world of black and white. An orange circle residing around a smiling gray walrus, from none other than Wally's Ice Cream Shop, my favorite place in this small town.

The piercing sounds of a scream rang through my ears. It was coming from me, my body disconnected from my mind once again.

Until I was overcome by a sea of black and the world disappeared before me.

ANDIE L. SMITH

Chapter Four

There is so much about that night I don't remember. So much I refuse to hear, refuse to accept. Now, staring back at the wooden door of my childhood home, I feel too many things all at once.

Anger. Fear. Desperation.

There's not enough room in my body to deal with any of those things.

As I reach the top of the stairs, I hear my mom murmuring to herself from down below. Seconds after I turn to look back at her, she's at the bottom of the stairs, smiling up at me and tightening her robe.

Sometimes I really think she might secretly be a ninja.

"Alex, is everything okay?" she asks me, rubbing away the sleep from her eyes.

"Everything's fine, Mom. I'm getting home from a party," I tell her.

"Oh, good, that's great, sweetie. I hope you had fun." She yawns through her words and walks off, back to her bedroom and what will probably be a deep sleep.

I head into my room with the same goal in mind and try not to let the fact that my own mother had no care about me being at a party this late crowd my thoughts. It's well after midnight, but she seems to care less about my whereabouts or my company.

This is pretty normal behavior for her, not caring about where I am. I didn't start noticing it until after I started hanging out with Paige and Becca, coming home after 2:00 in the morning and stumbling my way up the stairs half the time from drinking too much.

She would always check on me, ask me if everything was okay, and then go back to her room like nothing happened. A part of me is glad she isn't overbearing, especially since I watched her play the bad cop for most of my life towards my sister.

But another part of me is disappointed every time she goes back to her room. Sometimes I want her to yell at me, to accuse me of wasting my life away, to ground me, even give me a curfew that didn't allow me to come home in the wee hours of the morning.

I don't want to get in trouble, or even have her hate me, but... I don't know. Sometimes I want to get some sort of reaction out of her, to feel like she really does care about what happens to me. Like I wasn't some item she could discard to a secondhand store the moment something goes wrong.

After a much-needed shower, I braid back my hair and tie it off at the end. I climb into bed and pull my laptop close. Recognizable photos pop up immediately of tonight's party before it got busted. I scroll through Instagram to see pictures of my friends having fun, both with and without me. Some scenes make me laugh more than others, like seeing Becca's tongue shoved down Daniel Michelson's throat. *Those two are something else.*

I shut my laptop and toss it on the rug, knowing nothing I see will make the other feelings go away.

No matter how much I drink, no matter how many parties I go to, this aching feeling in my chest still won't leave. The continuous feeling of being suspended into the air and then dropping into a pit of nothing but darkness.

"Ugh," I blab out in my empty room.

My thoughts yet again get the better of me and as the clock reads 4:10 AM, I decide to go to sleep. All of my problems and complications will still be here in the morning, so I might as well be rested for them. *What a Friday night this has turned out to be.*

I turn off my bedside lamp and roll over,

spreading out underneath the fluffy, midnight blue duvet that covers my bed. Dozing off under my bamboo rose-colored sheets, I try to ignore the pain in my heart and drift off into a blissful patch of darkness.

****

"So today I was thinking we start by apologizing," Blaze says as we walk into our usual Saturday morning diner for brunch with the girls.

The Hipsty Diner is one of the many diners in Summersville, but all the same happens to be Blaze's and my favorite. At the beginning of freshman year, we had a diner challenge and drove around to every single diner in town to determine who had the best chocolate chip pancakes. We did this all in the span of one day, and by the end of it, I swore my pants were going to burst open at the seams. Hipsty was one of the last places we tried, and their pancakes put all others to shame a thousand times over.

We've been coming here every Saturday morning since, and even got Paige and Becca to join us.

I raise my eyebrow at Blaze as we climb into the comfort of our favorite booth at the back of the diner. Her face turns a shade of red that almost matches her hair.

I glance over at Paige and Becca, who looks like she's about to be sick.

"We're really sorry for ditching you last night. I didn't want to, but you know what my mom would do to me if I got caught at that party," Becca says in a rushed breath.

"Yeah, yeah, boarding school immediately followed by intense drug and alcohol rehab," I recite back to her in the best mom voice I can muster. "But it's fine, really. I'm the one who told you guys to go."

They all stare at me blankly, waiting for an explosion that never comes. Am I supposed to be mad?

"Guys, it's fine! Really. I didn't want to leave without Jordan. But turns out he must have found a ride, so I got out of there fairly quickly, even though I had to ride home in a dingy Honda Civic with some strange guy," I rush out the last part and sip my iced coffee the waitress brought over.

"Wait a second, *what*? You left with a rando! Alexandra Marsh, do spill your ever so-interesting beans," Becca laughs. *Yep, and he totally watched me fall apart like the cracks of the asphalt I was sitting on.*

As we eat, I fill them in on my not-so-exciting night with Cameron and don't forget to include the fact that he was actually pretty hot, and his jacket might have smelled more than amazing. I don't mention getting pulled over, or what took place afterward.

They laugh when they can, mostly through mouthfuls of fried dough and fresh fruit.

The entire time I notice how Paige's brow furrows, waiting to hear a part that doesn't come out of my mouth.

"So, did he walk you to your door? Did he kiss you goodnight?" Her eagerness gets the best of her.

Her tone is bitter. I don't like it.

I laugh. "No and no. Jeez, Paige, I just met him."

She rolls her eyes and opens her mouth to say something, but Blaze cuts her off.

"And you have a boyfriend, who you are happily in love with. Right?"

"Right. That." I smile at the girls, but don't expand on the thought.

I texted Jordan three times this morning, with no reply. At this very moment, no, I'm not very happy with him. He didn't even bother to ask if I made it home okay, or let me know he was good, wherever the hell he ended up.

"So, do you think you'll see him again?" Becca asks, once again turning the conversation back to Cameron.

"I doubt it. I don't even think he goes to our school," I point out. *I really hope he doesn't go to our school.*

"And you wouldn't do anything with him anyways, right? That V-card of yours is still very much intact." Paige nods at me. She shoves another forkful of berries into her mouth.

Blaze drops her knife onto her plate, the loud *clanging* sound ringing in my ears. Becca's mouth is wide open.

"What the hell is that supposed to mean?" I ask, confused at her tone, still so bitter.

"Nothing. It was a joke. Forget it." She waves me off, but by the way the other girls are looking at me, that's the last thing I want to do.

"That didn't sound like a joke. What did you mean by that, Paige?" I press her.

Paige doesn't like me. I know this. The first day I met her, she called me Jordan's "playmate." But despite her questionable looks and scoffs here and there, she left me alone... for the most part. Starting a scene like this in front of Becca and Blaze was new. I'm not sure how I feel about it. The two minutes it takes for her to chew and swallow her fruit feels like an eternity.

"It's nothing," she reaches across the table to grab a napkin and wipes at her mouth. "It's just, we all know you and Jordan still haven't slept together. I don't know what's taking so long, honestly. His last girlfriend gave it up after the first week of dating."

My jaw opens so wide it probably could've hit the floor if I was any shorter. I glance over at Blaze and Becca, their expressions matching my own.

"What?" Paige looks at all of us as if *we* are the ones who said something insane. "She did. And I know for a fact that you haven't."

"Are you serious?" I can't believe she's saying this. My sex life—or nonexistent sex life—is none of her business. Jordan and I are still new, too new for that.

"I'm just saying, at some point you need to figure your shit out. He's not going to wait around for you forever. You want to be with him, right?" She bites off a piece of turkey bacon from her plate.

I'm speechless. The words I want to say would be too cruel, even though she deserves them. My mouth remains shut. The desire to eat breakfast is gone. My eyes don't want to look at her anymore. I throw a twenty dollar bill down onto the table to pay for my meal. Shaking my head, I rise to my feet.

I storm out of the diner without another word to any of them. Paige is unbelievable. Everyone keeps telling me to "get my shit together" in one way or the other. My mom, my sister, Paige.

Paige acting like losing my virginity is as easy as my family moving on from my dad's death. The comparison makes my stomach churn.

It's bad enough I have to find a way to move forward without my father, now I'm supposed to give up my virginity, too?

I make it about halfway on my walk home before I realize something that slows my pace.

In Paige's inexcusable outburst and my quick exit, my anger got the best of me. She got exactly what she wanted—a reaction. And I didn't even answer her question.

I take a moment to ponder her question again, and what my answer would have been.

What my answer should have been.

Of course, I want to be with Jordan. I mean sure, am I still mad at him for leaving me last night and not even bothering to text me an explanation? Yes. Does he occasionally forget to include me in his plans or find me after his games? Also yes. But it isn't always like that, only over the last couple of weeks. We've both been busy with our teams and have an understanding about that.

That doesn't mean I don't want to be with him, don't *want* him. That doesn't mean I don't love him.

Does it?

As I continue walking, my mind begins to wander. I let it. I think about the night Jordan told me he loved me, and butterflies enter my stomach by letting the memory resurface.

"Ah!" I screamed and ducked my head into Jordan's chest.

I still don't know how I let him convince me to see a horror movie, everything about that night was absolutely terrifying.

Jordan chuckled as he wrapped his arms tighter around my shoulders. He put his hand over my eyes as if to shield me from the monsters roaming around the screen before us.

"It's not real, babe."

"I don't care! It's still scary!"

He laughed again and removed his hand, moving it underneath my chin and tipping my head up to meet his gaze.

His hazel eyes stared at my lips, and he brushed his tongue quickly over his own. I held my breath and waited for him to lean in. I knew he was about to kiss me.

Kissing Jordan felt like swimming laps around a pool. No, more like diving into the deep end and not being able to find your way back to the surface. We had only been dating for a few weeks, but I never got tired of kissing him. I got lost in it, in him, and I rarely ever wanted to come up for air.

"Okay, if we get to make out the whole time, then I'll see all the horror movies you want," I whispered to him when he pulled away.

He winked at me and quickly looked around the theater before reaching over to grab me by the waist. He hoisted me over the armrest sitting between us—stupid thing was locked in place and wouldn't lift up—and brought me into his lap, so that my legs were straddling either side of him.

The entire movement made my stomach flip, and I nervously looked around to see if anyone saw us.

"Jordan! We're in a theater!"

"There's like one other person watching this movie. And besides, we're in the back row. Everyone knows why couples always sit in the back row at a movie." He wrapped a hand around the base of my neck and pulled me closer to him.

A shiver ran down my back from his touch and my lips brushed against his. He kissed me softly and then pried my lips open with his tongue, finding mine and encircling it as if he was tracing all the tiny bumps that coat the top.

My whole body felt warm and tingly, and I realized I had no idea what I was doing. I've kissed other boys before Jordan, but those were little pecks and most were on a dare or because of a game of spin the bottle. Those kisses were nothing like the ones I shared with him.

"I love you," he whispered against my breath.

It was so soft, I almost didn't hear it over the screams of the girl in the movie being butchered by the zombie that was following her. That was the last horror movie I would ever see.

"What?" I wanted to make sure I heard him correctly.

"I love you," he said again.

His smile was so wide, it sent his mismatched dimples halfway to his ears.

Surprise was my first reaction. Relief followed.

I had wanted to say the words to him for a few days but was nervous at how he would react. He was Jordan Tucker after all, a lot of girls have told him they love him. But I wanted him to know that I meant it. That when I said it, it was special.

"I love you, too." I wrapped my arms around the back of his neck and kissed him with a newfound sense of urgency.

We walked out of the movie, the kids at the ticket booth snickering at us.

My smile could have lit up the whole town.

It didn't leave my face when Jordan dropped me off and I went to bed that night. The next morning, it was still there when I ran into his arms in the school hallway. Everyone stared, some people laughed, and some girls whispered, cursing my name under their breath. I didn't care.

I couldn't believe it.

Jordan Tucker said he loved me.

Another memory pops into my mind—Jordan taking me roller skating.

"Jordan! I can't slow down!" I screamed after he pushed me forward, the wheels on my skates propelled faster against wood flooring.

He caught up to me so fast, I wasn't sure how he did it. Roller skating was not something I was good at. Jordan's hand wrapped around my waist and he brought me over to the wall, pushed me against the edge and leaned into me. The familiar scent of sweat and aftershave overwhelmed me.

For a moment it felt like we were the only ones out there on the rink.

My heart would flutter at the way he would stare at me. Like he was trying to find the missing piece to a ten-year-old puzzle.

When he was with me, he was different. Someone other than the popular guy who had a reputation to uphold. The version of Jordan I got to see was special, unique, a secret I wanted to keep to myself forever.

Those moments were precious. When glimpses of the real Jordan came out so briefly, so distinctly. Standing there, trying not to slip on the wheels tied to my feet and staring into his hazel eyes, I was with the real Jordan. The one who wanted to have fun and kiss his girlfriend until his lips turned red.

I loved that Jordan.

Even when being with him felt too good to be true.

Chapter Five

Right at the halfway mark between my house and The Hipsty Diner, is an old recreation center the town used to frequently overpopulate. The center lives on Lake Monroe, which is really more of a pond if the size is analyzed correctly.

Not that we have many lakes in Summersville, but I always thought of this one as my own little personal hideout. It isn't nearly as big as Summersville Lake, where everyone went to cliff dive or tube and hang out during the summer.

The open field of grass where I'm standing now used to be an enormous parking lot, back when this place was an actual park that people brought their kids to. To the right of the parking lot, there used to be a huge playground structure that was made of wood, with pillars shaped like turrets of a castle and lanky bridges connecting the entire thing throughout the forest. It was set on silky white sand and there were so many different ways you could play—the tire swing, the elevated seesaw, or even the rotating monkey bars.

My dad and I used to come here all the time. It was our Saturday tradition.

Of course, that was *before*.

Little Alex used to climb all over the thing, through so many tunnels I lost count—and I tried to count how many there were so many times.

My favorite part was going underneath the entire structure to get to the other side as fast as I could. It was like a wooden maze. The absolute best place to play hide and seek. If it weren't for always getting hungry every hour and needing a snack, I never would have come out of my hiding places.

"*Alex! Come on! It's time to go,*" my dad yelled out at me.

"*No! I don't want to go home!*" I yelled back.

I ran through the tunnels under the castle structure, chasing other kids as I went. If I stayed under there forever, no one would ever find me.

"*Gotcha!*" my dad screamed as his hands wrapped around my small torso.

Screams and giggles left my mouth as he tickled me underneath the castle. He scooped me up before I could even blink and soon enough, we made our way back to the car.

"*Dad! I want to keep playing,*" I begged.

"*I know sweetie, but your mom has dinner ready. We can come back next weekend,*" he said.

"*Do you promise?*" I looked at him.

"*I promise,*" he replied.

"*I want to come back every weekend!*" I screamed as he buckled me into the backseat.

"*We can come back every weekend for as long as you want.*" He smiled at me.

For as long as I want, I remember thinking.

"*One day, I'm going to get married here,*" I told him as he backed out of the parking lot.

Jenna and I had started playing 'wedding' back then. The idea of getting married was so cool to me, even though I didn't really understand what it meant. Being five or six years old, I was allowed to dream.

"*You are not allowed to get married until you are at least 30, and I doubt at that age you will want to be married in a wooden playpark surrounded by children,*" my dad laughed at me.

"*But I want to get married in the sand!*" I exclaimed.

"*Then go to the beach.*" He winked at me through

the rearview mirror and began our drive home.

A beach wedding. Now that was a dream.

The memory makes me smile, but it also ignites the ever-growing ache inside my chest. My eyes continue to glaze over my surroundings. At how much has changed in a space that meant so much to me.

Next to the wooden playground on the left was a beautiful field with gazebos arranged in a circle. Regular park-goers would use them to eat their picnic lunches, or even to throw birthday parties. The park was built to be as close to the lake as possible. Back then, the dock was open for business for people to use for boating, jet skiing, or casual day fishing. If you had your birthday party here, you were pretty much the coolest kid in the class.

Now, though, everything is gone. The wooden structure was torn down years ago for safety reasons. All that remains is the sand, which is now covered up by overgrown weeds. The gazebos still stood, although most of them were so rotted down no one dared to go near them. Well, no one really came here anymore, so I guess it's me who didn't dare go near them.

The lake is still here. After my dad died, this place became my solace. I found myself coming down here almost every weekend to sit by the water. My dad loved the water.

"Alex?" a voice snaps me out of my daze.

For a moment, I forgot why I'm here. Paige, the diner, the outburst. Questioning my love for Jordan.

Oh, right, that.

My eyes find the source of the interruption. It's Cam, the boy from last night. *Oh, no.* This could not be happening. *What is he doing here?*

"Are you following me?" I question him.

He holds his hands up as if to say he comes in peace. "What? No. I was walking by and I saw you. You looked upset, so I wanted to see if you were okay."

My anger softens at his words, so caring. So kind. But it's misplaced, I don't deserve it. I don't want it. I can't stand to see the pity in his eyes one more time. So I let my anger towards Paige resurface, and I direct it at him.

"I'm fine, and I don't need you checking on me. I have a boyfriend, you know."

"Right, the mysterious Jordan Tucker. Who is such a great boyfriend, he leaves you alone at a party to get busted by the cops." He crosses his arms and a playful smile forms on his lips.

Okay, that pisses me off. Now my anger towards him is real.

"And let me guess, you're a real stand-up guy yourself?" I match his stance.

"I'm a better man than one who leaves his girl alone at a party. You never know who she could meet." He winks at me.

Despite my best efforts, my stomach flips at the action. It takes me a moment to remember why I'm mad at him. I don't really have a reason—besides not wanting him to out me for being a complete and total freak—but some part of me knows he's bad news.

"You really don't know who Jordan Tucker is?" I ask in disbelief. Even if this guy is homeschooled, he should know the town's most popular quarterback.

His only response is a shrug and that same lopsided grin I saw last night. The butterflies come back. I try to push them away.

"Star quarterback at Woodbridge? Most popular guy at school? Do you even go there?" *Please say no.*

"I go to Woodbridge," he answers only one of my questions and not in the way I wanted.

Now it's my turn to shrug, and I look at him

expectantly.

"What? I don't keep up with all that crap." He waves his hand in the air.

"What crap?"

"That popular bullshit. Dating the football quarterback. Dressing like someone else. Acting like you are better than everyone. It's not my scene." He stares at me and my irritation increases.

His eyes rake over my body and like last night, I feel my skin ignite at every surface of skin he covers.

"You don't know anything about me, jerk."

He walks closer to me. With every step he takes, my chest tightens. His face is only inches away from mine. It's like I forgot how to breathe.

"I know more about you than you think," his voice is calmer now, sadder.

He's talking about last night, about what happened to me. What did he call it? A panic attack. No, I'm not the kind of girl that gets panic attacks. My mouth parts to tell him as much when the words get caught in my throat. His stare is agonizing. As if he's trying to convey some sort of secret message I'm supposed to understand. Only then do I notice the color of his eyes for the first time. Blue, but flaked with a contrast of emerald green so deep it's like staring into the ocean.

My skin continues to burn under his gaze.

His eyes briefly drop down to my lips. The movement is so fast, blinking would have caused me to miss it. But I don't blink.

A rush of heat flows through my body and I feel my face redden.

"What are you doing?" I push him away.

Immediately, my body aches at the distance between us. *Stop it*, I attempt to will it. I don't know this boy. There is no need to be reacting to him this way.

He really is bad news.

"N-nothing," he stutters as if our proximity caught him off guard as well.

"Who even are you? What do you want from me?" I press him.

"I don't want anything from you. Sorry, I'll go." He shakes his head and starts to walk off toward the main road.

He turns back around to look at me and chuckles when he catches me staring after him. I blush at the embarrassment and watch his figure fade into the distance. The breath I was holding when he brought his face to mine releases. My body shivers at the recollection of his stare.

I don't know what it was, but it was almost like he was trying to tell me something without having to say anything at all. And there was something else in his eyes that I couldn't quite put my finger on but I swear I've seen before.

Walking home, I can't shake the thought that Cam really was trying to tell me something. Was it something about Jordan? Was he in trouble? Or worse, did he tell him about last night?

Ridiculous. Cameron said himself he doesn't know Jordan.

My thoughts provoke me to check my phone as I head through the front door and up the stairs to my bedroom, but I roll my eyes when the thread with my boyfriend comes up empty, save for my last few messages, still unanswered.

My emotions change. What should be worry and fear is overtaken by frustration and anger.

The cold water of my bathroom sink calls to me. Splashing some on my face, I try to collect myself. Taking deep breaths, my hands grasp for a towel to dry off my face. The towel falls away, and I'm glancing at my reflection in the mirror. Normally, I don't stare at myself for longer than a minute. I know what I look like, and that's pretty average compared to my friends. But looking back at myself now, I catch something I haven't seen there before.

Something familiar, like a book I read many years ago and know the premise of, but can't remember any of the minor details.

I gasp. The towel drops to the floor. The recognition is overwhelming.

There, in the reflection of my dark, brown eyes, a hint of something so small you wouldn't notice it at first glance.

But I do. Because I saw the same speck of it perfectly reflected in someone else's eyes.

Eyes I looked into only a few moments ago.

A mark of tragedy.

****

"Do you need more time, sweetie?" my mom asked me.

The grassy field of the cemetery was eerie. My legs itched from the nine ant bites I had gotten while being there. But I couldn't bring my feet to move.

It had been two weeks since my dad died, one since the funeral. Sleep never came. My appetite was gone. There wasn't much I was able to do.

"Can I have a few more minutes? You can wait for me in the car if you want," I said to her.

My mom smiled and patted my shoulder, relieved to be walking away from the sight before us. As if she couldn't walk away fast enough.

My eyes looked back over to the stone lying in the ground. No matter which way I looked at it, those words stuck out to me. They were holographically hovering in the air above me, not engraved into a rock buried into the ground.

Benjamin Marsh
Loving Father of Jenna and Alexandra
May 13, 1973—April 7, 2022

The grave was placed under a large oak tree. It would provide a nice blanket of shade during the summer heat. A thick, concrete bench sat under the tree, but it too was covered with ants at the time. My legs were already bitten, but I still didn't want to sit down.

Ever since the funeral, I wanted to come here. Begged my mom to take me. The headstone wasn't ready yet, she would say to me. I had never seen a headstone before, didn't know what one would look like.

Google did me no favors—there were apparently too many choices. Ones that were flat and laid into the ground, others that sat tall and upright in a large oval shape. There were even some in an actual tomblike house structure, and I wondered what kinds of people were buried in those.

One week later, the headstone was ready. It was in front of me now, but I didn't want to look at it.

I couldn't look away.

If I stared at it long enough, I thought I could try to change the words. To erase my dad's name and add someone else's. But that wouldn't do anything about the fact that it was his body lying in the ground beneath my feet.

The tears I waited for never came.

My mom's words from the funeral came back to my mind, the final action to be done with all of this. It wasn't the funeral for me, it was standing here. Seeing the black and gray stone in front of me. This was the moment I needed, the last thing on my checklist to cross off so I could be free. I had been looking forward to this moment.

But still, the tears didn't come. There was no anger, no confusion. There wasn't much of anything. My chest felt as empty and hollow as the chocolate Easter eggs my parents used to buy us every April.

April. The month stood out to me on the stone. There was no satisfaction, only disappointment. Would Jenna ever come here? Would I come back?

I wasn't sure if I wanted to return to my father's place of rest.

The words felt funny in my mind—a place of rest. Like my dad was going to bed for a really long time. He was going to sleep forever, sure, but it's not like it was his choice. Not like he said goodnight to all of us and decided not to wake up the next day.

This wasn't his place of rest.

This was his place of death.

The fake bouquet of flowers in my hand felt heavy as I placed them neatly in the little ceramic vase at the center of the stone. Spreading out the groups of their buds so they fanned over the headstone like leaves of a palm tree.

My mom assured me the caretakers would water real flowers, but they weren't the ones I wanted. "Never pay anyone to take care of something so dear to your heart, they won't do it right," her words about her garden ring in my ears. The caretakers weren't what bothered me. It was the irony of the situation.

Putting something alive and growing in a place that only marked death and finality.

The rhododendrons stared back at me, a set that carried the orange and red hues of a sunset. It was the West Virginia state flower, and my dad's favorite. He loved watching the sunset over the water. The colors were fitting, a perfect choice for a bouquet that would stay here with him forever.

Forever. What an awfully long time.

The walk back to the car was quick, my mom in the front seat, dancing along as an ABBA song played over the radio. As if she was out for a casual drive, not visiting her husband's grave.

My seatbelt clicked into place at the same time something locked inside my chest. It was as if something was shutting off. A key frame being secured into position.

My mom drove away. I gave one last look to the space that held my dad's grave.

His body. The place he would remain forever.

Unaware if I would ever see it again.

Unsure if I even wanted to return.

Chapter Six

"Mom, can I ask you something?"

The radio quiets, and my mother brushes a strand of hair back behind her ear. Unlike my wavy mane, hers is thin and straight. She keeps it relatively short, sitting above her shoulders. Though it used to be the same color of brown as mine and Jenna's, hers is now dyed a bright shade of blonde. It contrasts her green eyes stunningly, and makes her look serious almost all the time. I always wondered how much of that had to do with her job, or her personality in general.

My mother is gorgeous. Sometimes it hurts to look at her. But it's always more difficult to look away.

We're driving home from the grocery store after getting a bundle of things completely unrelated to the usual grocery items a family would need in the house.

She's having her monthly book club meeting tonight, and it's her turn to host. If my mom loves anything more than her career, it's hosting events. I don't even know how she found the time for it, but somehow she did. And every time, she goes all out.

Our house goes from a casual homey environment to an elegant networking space. She hangs string lights all around the living room, and pushes the furniture together in a way that has the couch and loveseats forming a perfect U-shape around the center coffee table.

Each time they meet, her book club themes the food around whatever it is they are reading that month. Since we are riding home with bags full of pineapples and pina colada mixes, I can only assume they are reading some sort of summer romance novel.

"Of course, sweetie," she answers me.

"Why don't we ever go visit Dad?"

My question catches her off guard, and she brakes the car so fast I'm scared for a moment the one behind us is going to slam right into her back bumper. My body catches on the seat belt and is forced back into the seat.

"Ouch!" I cry.

"S-sorry, Alex," she mutters. "I didn't know that's what you were going to ask."

I wait for a moment, but she continues to drive and doesn't answer me.

"Well?" I ask again.

"I'm not sure what you mean, dear. We can't visit your dad. He's gone. You know that."

There's a strain in her voice. The whites of her knuckles are visible as she tightens her grip on the steering wheel.

"Right," I say, totally perplexed by that response. "But I meant visiting his grave."

"Oh, Alex, we don't need to do that." She shakes her head and waves her hand in the air like she's smelled something bad. *We don't?*

I open my mouth to speak, but she interrupts me. Which is probably for the best because honestly, I'm not sure what I was going to say in the first place.

"We already saw the grave. There's no reason to go see it again."

Her words send a thousand thoughts through my mind, and I don't know which one to pinpoint and say out loud.

I remember when a girl in my fourth grade class missed school for an entire week, because her grandpa had died. We all gave her flowers and a card the whole class signed when she came back to school. She looked sad, but our gifts had made her smile.

The next year, I noticed she was in my class again. I went up to her on the playground and asked her if she missed her grandpa.

I didn't know how death worked back then, how final it all was. Not sure death will be something I ever understand, even now.

"A lot," she said to me. "But I get to visit and talk to him all the time, so it's okay."

I remember looking around scared for a minute, like her dead grandpa's ghost was haunting the playground. I had never seen a ghost before, but I knew they were real. I had ridden the Haunted Mansion enough times at Disney World to know the difference.

"Not here, stupid," she said when she noticed me looking around.

I asked her what she meant and she told me that every month, she and her mom would go visit his grave at the cemetery. They would bring a blanket and sometimes snacks, and they would sit there and talk for hours. To each other, to her grandpa.

"But he isn't there, is he?" I had asked her. Again, having thoughts about ghosts.

"Of course he is!" she snapped at me and walked off from her spot on the swings.

That was the last time I talked to her.

For a while, I definitely thought she was talking to her grandpa's ghost. When my dad died, I hoped for a moment that his afterlife form would materialize and he would get to stay with me forever.

But he never showed.

I stare back at my mom now as we pull into the house, and her entire face has changed. A moment ago, she looked worried, scared even. But when I didn't say anything more about the subject of my dad's grave, she turned the radio back up and a huge smile returned to her face. *Her and this damn radio.*

All I want is to be able to talk to my dad the way

that girl in my class could talk to her grandpa. And to do that, I need to visit his grave.

When we saw it after the funeral, a part of me wondered if we would ever go back to see it again. I assumed so, I mean, why wouldn't we?

I really thought my mom had been waiting for me to ask and then once I did, she would happily go with me. Sure, I don't *need* her to take me. I can drive to the cemetery myself. But something about doing that scares the hell out of me.

I don't want to go alone, and I don't want to bring Jordan along or even Blaze. But if my mom doesn't want to go, I'm sure I know one other person who may want to go with me.

We head inside the house. I finish helping her unload the groceries, excusing myself upstairs to freshen up for the party tonight. My door shuts and I pull out my phone, already pressing the "call" button on my sister's contact card.

"Alex, is everything okay?" Jenna asks.

"All good, I just had a question for you."

"Okay, what is it?"

"Would you want to come with me to visit Dad?"

****

My head is pounding. The blood in my face is throbbing in my cheeks, my ears.

The bass is *thrumping* against my feet and I clutch my red cup expectantly, waiting for Jordan to make himself known. It's Saturday night, and even though I'm still mad at Paige for her little outburst at breakfast, that wasn't going to stop me from coming to a party.

We're at Daniel Michelson's house tonight—Becca's ongoing on-again-off-again boyfriend. Frankly, I don't know what she sees in him. He got kicked off the football team at the beginning of the year for smoking pot, and he isn't much of a brain in any of his classes either. He dresses like a skater boy, heavy oversized clothing and always smells like he hasn't put on deodorant in days. Regardless of his appearance, his house is huge.

His mom is some hot shot Congress member, and is always flying out to D.C. for work, so she's never home. I have no idea what Daniel's dad does, if he's even around in the first place. The thought makes me sad for him, and I almost feel bad for judging him so harshly. But the moment passes as soon as he runs through the kitchen screaming and holding a red cup high in the air, wearing nothing but a pool floatie around his waist—shaped as a duck, no less.

I shake my head and look over at Becca, who's staring after him dreamily. She laughs when she looks back at me and shrugs as if to say, 'what are you going to do?'

I'm happy for her, she clearly loves him enough to deal with his crazy antics. Thoughts of Jordan cloud my mind, not sure if I can say the same.

"Hey," Paige's harsh tone overtakes the blood throbbing in my ears before I even turn around to face her.

As always, she looks gorgeous. Her blue bodycon dress is so tight against her skin, showing off every outline of her curves through the thin material.

The romantic part of my brain wonders how many boys are going to turn their heads at her tonight. The logical part of my brain wonders how in the hell she's wearing underwear under that thing, but then I think better of it.

She probably isn't wearing any at all.

I can't help but feel bland in comparison, my yellow halter top and jean skirt selling myself short.

"Hi." I stare at her. My anger is still settled low in my stomach, and there's no need to act like it isn't.

"Don't be mad, Lex. I said I was sorry."

I blink at her in confusion, trying to recall some moment she thinks I so clearly forgot about. She never said she was sorry.

"I don't remember hearing you apologize," I say to her.

"Well, I did. So you can't be mad anymore."

Oh, I can't?

Her attitude is really something. If I wasn't with Jordan, I know for a fact that this girl and I would never be friends out of our own desires. I'm not even sure we're friends now. It feels like we're constantly walking on eggshells around each other, patiently waiting for one of us to scream from the pain against our feet.

But I'm not going to be the one to crack first.

Her phone goes off in her hand and I watch as she pulls it up to her chest quickly so that it's out of my view. But she isn't fast enough, a glimpse of the contact that texted her visible out of the corner of my eye. "J" with a red heart next to the letter. I can't make out the message, but whatever it is has Paige smiling and blushing so brightly, it's starting to create contrast against her blue dress.

"I need to go." She gets rid of her smile, but looks at me with condescending eyes and places her hand on my arm briefly. "But I'm so glad we talked and worked everything out, you're such an understanding friend."

I blink to myself a few times as I watch her walk away, heading up the back staircase of the house. *What was that about?*

"What the hell happened there?" Blaze comes up from behind me and starts pouring a bottle of store-brand vodka into my cup. I take a big swig and flinch, the clear liquid burning down the back of my throat.

"I have absolutely no idea," I say to her. We both start laughing as she goes to fill my cup up again.

Paige's fake apology gets under my skin, and makes me even more angry than I was before I came to this party. I take a long sip of the refilled vodka in my cup and think over my phone call with Jenna earlier.

"What do you mean visit Dad?" she asked me.

"What is it with you and Mom not understanding that question?" I scoffed in frustration. "I mean go visit his grave. Have you even been there at all?"

"No, I haven't. And I don't need to. Why do you want to go to his grave?"

"Why don't you? Don't you want to visit him, talk to him, say goodbye or say anything at all? You didn't even go to the funeral!"

"Alex, I don't know why you are yelling at me, but I don't have time for this," my sister snapped.

"Are you serious? You couldn't be bothered to come to the funeral, and now you can't be bothered to visit your father's grave? Who are you?" I yelled through frantic tears.

"Stop being so dramatic, Alex. You know who I am."

"No, I don't think I do," I said before I hung up on her.

She tried to call me back three times. Each and every one of her calls went to voicemail.

I had nothing more to say to her. I couldn't believe she was acting that way.

Between both her and my mom acting like *I* was the crazy one for wanting to visit Dad's grave, I'm starting to feel that way. Am I being crazy? Is there really no point in going to see the place where he's buried?

Again, I think about the girl in my class from

fourth grade. How happy she was when she told me she gets to talk to her grandpa all the time. My heart clenches. I want that. I *need* that. Why can't anyone see that?

Blaze tugs on my arm and pulls me back to the scene at the party. She leads me out onto the makeshift dance floor, which is really the center of the living room cleared out—the couches and other items of furniture pushed back against the wall.

It's a large space, but with all the bodies crowding it, it feels like the size of a closet. People are bumping into me left and right, and I keep trying to strain my neck over the crowd to look at the front door, thinking Jordan is going to walk in any minute.

Blaze and I dance for a few songs and finish off the bottle of vodka in her hand.

I'm starting to feel good, and almost forget about the fact that my boyfriend isn't here dancing with me. When a random guy brushes past me and winks at me, I feel my skin start to heat up. *Jordan is missing out.*

I head into the kitchen to grab another bottle for me and Blaze when a tall figure with dirty-blonde spiky hair catches my eye heading up the back staircase. For a moment, I swear it's Jordan.

The figure disappears up the stairs almost as quickly as he showed up. Laughter escapes my lips, the alcohol in my veins tricking me. The thought pushes me to check, but my phone still shows no new messages or missed calls from my boyfriend.

It's weird, but he must be busy doing something with the football team. An extra practice, or late night study session to come up with plays or something for the homecoming game. He's always postponing our dates for the football guys. Surely, that has to be where he is now. Because if Jordan really was at this party, he would be drinking and dancing with me.

Not hanging out upstairs with random people I don't know.

I bring the bottle back over to Blaze and we drink about a quarter of it before we both tap out. At this point the room is spinning and I'm not sure which way is the front or the back of the house. My face feels hot and I'm starting to get claustrophobic.

I watch Becca and Daniel making out in the corner of the room, the duck shaped pool floatie still around his waist. The vodka swirls in my stomach, desperately trying to find a way out.

"I don't feel so good," I say and grab onto Blaze's arm.

"Come on." Blaze pulls me away. "Let's go get some fresh air."

We step out onto the patio, though I'm not sure how Blaze managed to figure out which door was the back of the house, and a cool breeze welcomes us. Drinking always makes my face get red and body hot, and that's one of the worst parts for me. That, and the way my stomach wants me to relive the night and all my bad decisions the next morning.

I take a deep breath and feel a breeze wrap around my bare legs. The West Virginia weather is finally starting to cool down, and I'm thankful for the reprieve the chilly night air gives me. We sit down on the brick patio and kick off our shoes, sticking our feet into the pool. I wince at the hot water—of course Daniel has a heated pool.

"No Jordan tonight?" Blaze asks me.

"I haven't seen him."

"Trouble in paradise?" she laughs.

I know she's joking, but I can't bring myself to laugh with her. Jordan isn't returning my calls or texts. I have no idea what he's up to or where he ended up last night. *Or who he ended up with.* The thought makes my stomach churn and again I suppress the urge to empty the vodka onto my lap.

"Whoa, I was kidding," Blaze taps my arm lightly. "Are things really not okay?"

I kick my feet in the warm water. "I don't even know what 'okay' means anymore."

"Did he do something?"

I shrug at her. The truth is, Jordan hasn't really done anything. But that's kind of the problem. There's nothing wrong... except for him not replying to me today, but something is still upsetting me. I can't figure out what it is.

"No, it's that I—" I start to say.

Screams from the backyard grab my attention, and I see a group of football players running up behind us. One very large guy tosses a ball into the air and then jumps into the pool after it. Instantly, Blaze and I are soaking wet from the splash of a six foot three man child.

"Are you kidding me!" Blaze screams and gets to her feet.

"Oops—sorry!" the boy yells over to her.

I don't know why, but I find the whole thing hilarious. I start cracking up and am suddenly too high off my own laughter to even be mad that my clothes are soaking wet. Even though the water is warm, it's oddly refreshing for my sour state.

"Should we jump in?" I wiggle my eyebrows at Blaze.

"Seriously?"

"Why not? We're already wet." I take my feet out of the water and walk over to the deeper end of the pool.

"Oh, hell, yea! Lex is getting in!" I hear a guy scream.

"Lex, come on. Do you really want to do this?"

"Blaze, it's a pool. Don't be such a party pooper."

I push off the brick pathway and jump into the air, landing in a splash of heated chlorine and Styrofoam noodles. Warm water penetrates my skin as I'm submerged. It feels too good, too welcoming. For a moment I don't know if I can swim up to the surface. Or if I even want to.

My chest starts to burn for oxygen and I make my way to the top of the water.

The rest of the football team jumps in after I do, and before I know it, someone brought a set of speakers onto the porch to blast the music from the party inside. With all the guys in my vision, I do a quick survey, but still don't see Jordan. If the football team is here, then where is he?

Out of the corner of my eye, I see a figure in the window above the pool move away from the curtain so quickly, it could have been a ghost. If I wasn't looking around, I may not have even noticed it in the first place. But the swaying curtain in the upstairs window confirms what I see.

Someone's up there, and they're watching us.

****

It was sixth grade, and I had started middle school at Huntington Academy, a private school my mom was so happy I got into.

I was terrified of not making any friends and being made fun of. I didn't want to go to Huntington, but my mom promised I could go to the public high school if I really ended up hating it here.

The idea of being away from Blaze, my best friend, was torturous. She wasn't coming to Huntington, she was staying at the public middle school with all of our other friends.

My mom, my dad, and I were headed to my new school for Sneak Peek, an orientation to meet your teachers and sign up for clubs before school started the following week.

My mom was advocating for me to join the drama club, or the yearbook team, neither of which sounded that fun to me.

While we were taking a tour of the gym, a few kids were kicking a soccer ball around in a circle while their parents were talking in the opposite corner. Someone must have overestimated their kicking power, and the ball rolled over to us, landing right in front of my mom's feet.

"Some of these parents need to teach their children manners!" my mom hushed under her breath and stepped around the ball.

The kids were staring at me and motioning for me to give the ball back to them. I took a chance and kicked a perfect shot right into one of the older girl's hands. They all stared at me for a moment too long before going back to playing their game.

I must have been smiling, because my dad leaned down and said, "you know, women soccer players are pretty badass."

"Ben! Language!" my mom yelled as she smacked his arm.

"What! It's true. And Lexie, you can join any team or any club you want to, know that," he said.

My parents started arguing… they had been doing that a lot lately. I didn't want to hear it, so I jogged over to where the other kids were standing, still kicking the soccer ball around in a circle.

"Hi. I'm Alex," I said to them.

"I'm Martha," the older girl replied.

She pointed to each kid and said their name, but

there were so many that I instantly forgot who was who.

"Are you coming here this year?" a boy, Jack, I think, asked me.

"I think so," I nodded at them. "Maybe I'll join the soccer team."

The girls laughed at me and kept kicking the ball between them, almost like they were avoiding letting me touch it.

"What?" I asked them.

"You can't join the soccer team on a whim, Huntington only takes real players. Maybe try a rec team or something," Martha said to me.

I didn't like the way her nose turned up when she said rec team. Or what she meant by real players.

I ran over to my dad, tears streaming down so hard I could barely breathe.

"Lexie, what is it? What happened?"

"Those girls," I pointed over to the group, who were still laughing and kicking the ball around.

"They said I can't join the soccer team. That I'm not a real player."

"Alex, that's okay. You don't need to join the soccer team. There are so many other clubs and teams at the school you can be a part of. Ones that don't involve sweating and harsh injuries," my mom assured me.

"But—but I want to play soccer!" I cried.

My dad leaned down and hugged me tightly, whispering in my ear. "Then you play soccer. You and I will practice every day, and when you try out for the team, you will make it. And you will show those girls what you're made of."

I stared at him when he pulled me out of his hug. "You promise?"

"I swear on the rest of my life."

The scene changes—a gymnasium floor

becoming a field of grass.

A whistle blows and my ears ring from my close proximity to the sound.

"Foul!" the referee screams.

This is the third foul the ref has called on us in the entire first half. And like all the other calls, it's complete and total bullshit.

We're playing the South Carolina Tigers, a team so new we should be able to beat them with our eyes closed. Instead, there are ten minutes left in the game and the score is tied.

I could tell that everyone in the stands is on the edge of their seats. I quickly scan the crowd, trying to spot the one person who said he would be here. My tightened chest relaxes at the sight of him. I shouldn't have been worried.

My dad never missed a game.

He stands up and waves at me, throwing his arm around so wildly in the air he almost hits the lady sitting next to him in the face. I try not to laugh and pull my attention back to the field.

We need to score one more goal in the next few minutes to win this thing. One more goal, and we are that much closer to qualifying for the championship.

After a battle with the other team near our goal, my teammate Kenzie finally gets the ball.

"Over here!" I scream at her.

She passes it over to me, and I take off.

The world shuts out around me. Suddenly, I can't hear the screams of the crowd or the cheers of my teammates. I don't see the girls of the opposite team rushing towards me, trying to get the ball from under my feet. I completely tune out my surroundings. It's only me and the ball.

It's always like this when I play. I can't describe

it, this overwhelming feeling that I am connected to something bigger than I know.

My dad says it will make me a great player, that being able to focus and zone in so easily will help me stand out among the other girls on the team. He says I will be a star in no time.

That's exciting, the idea of being a star. But it also doesn't matter to me that much. I don't care about being a star, I only care about playing the game.

That's what I'm doing now, playing the game.

I run down the field with a new sense of urgency, knowing in the back of my mind the clock is ticking down. I need that perfect shot, and there is only enough time for one chance.

When one of my teammates blocks a girl who is running up along my right side, my opportunity presents itself.

The goalie is bouncing on her heels, back and forth, left and right, as my legs barrel their way down the right side of the field. Her mind is probably racing the same way mine is, calculating five hundred possible moves I can make in the span of one second. But I use that to play in my favor. I run forward, slightly to the left of the goal, and take my shot.

At the direction my body was facing, the goalie thinks I'm going to shoot left. She jumps in that direction, her arms spread out wide as she hits the ground, but never makes contact with the ball.

Because while my body is facing left, my legs have slightly shifted to the right, where I send the ball flying in the upper right hand corner of the net. Bodies start crashing into me as I jump into the air. My teammates are surrounding me in one giant hug, screaming and crying and laughing.

I shot the game-winning goal. And it feels

amazing.

We celebrate together on the field for a few more moments before we walk off to the locker rooms, singing "We Are the Champions" all the way to our showers. We know we're probably tempting fate, but we don't care.

I come out of the locker room and look around for that same person I wanted to see so badly during the game.

"There's my superstar!" I hear my dad yell as he comes into view.

"Dad, please don't call me that! Everyone can hear you." I'm embarrassed.

But I secretly love being his superstar.

"Sorry, sweetie. I'm so proud of you." He shakes his head at me. "And that goal! How did you fool the goalie like that?"

"I made her think I was going one way, when I was really going the other," I shrug.

"Genius. You are such a genius!" He kisses the top of my head and grabs my gym bag, slinging it over his shoulder.

"Genius enough to get two chocolate chip sandwiches tonight?" I smile wide at him.

"Why not?" My dad smiles back at me and wraps an arm around my shoulder as we walk to the car. "You only live once, right? Is that what you kids are saying these days?"

I roll my eyes at him. He's always doing this, trying to keep up with the crazy lingo of us teenagers.

"We may say that, but you definitely cannot," I laugh at him.

"Fine, I don't like the saying anyways. Whatever happened to swag? Swag was cool." He climbs into the front seat and I practically fall into the passenger side, the effects of the game already taking their toll on my *body.*

"Nobody says swag anymore, Dad."

"Coolio? Fetch?" he asks me.

I shake my head at him and bust out into a fit of laughter. This was going to be a long night.

I wake up abruptly and for a moment am not sure where I am. There's someone next to me in my bed—*was that Jenna?* But as my eyes adjust to the darkness of my room, I see her fiery red hair sticking out from under the blue comforter.

My bed, my house. Blaze next to me.

My breath catches at the realization. The back of my throat aches and burns at the intake of breath, and I almost burst into a coughing fit. Not wanting to wake Blaze, I quietly peel the covers off my legs and tiptoe my way down the stairs.

After pouring a glass of water and downing the whole thing in one gulp, I refill the Brita pitcher and place it back in the fridge. The coolness of the tile floor against my bare feet grounds me for a moment. My memory recalls the dreams that woke me in the first place.

That night at Sneak Peak felt like so long ago, like it was another life. Another Alex.

One who was happy, who had her dad back.

That night meant so much to me. I was so excited to find something I could be really good at. Determined to make my parents proud of me, a need to tell those mean girls to shove it.

My dad held his promise—he and I practiced almost every day. He said I was a natural, and only had to tweak a few things in the way I held myself over the ball, the position of my foot when I shot a goal, or how to block with my arms. He taught me everything I know.

I made the team in sixth grade and never looked

back. My mom ended up losing a big client she had halfway through the school year, so I didn't return to Huntington for seventh grade. I joined Blaze at the public middle school.

Now in high school, soccer continues to be the one thing I look forward to in my life. We play Huntington every year and Martha always acts like she has no idea who I am. But I always remembered her. The girl who told me I couldn't do something, giving me the drive and motivation to do exactly that.

I didn't know it at the time, but that day at Sneak Peak was the day I fell in love with soccer. And the day that my dad and I shared something we would never have with anyone else.

And that second dream, it wasn't a bad one, and for that I'm grateful. I love thinking about my dad, remembering some of my favorite moments with him. I wish I could talk about those moments with others.

Soccer is a huge part of my memories, I know that. I'm glad I haven't stopped playing even after he died. It feels different when I play now, sure. But it's still a part of me and I know my dad wouldn't want me to let that part go. Considering everything, the sport is one of the only ways I still feel connected to him. It used to be me and the ball on the field. But now it's always me, the ball, and my dad.

I head back upstairs and climb into bed, Blaze still sleeping soundly on the other side. Laying back down against my pillow, I let myself fall back asleep and wait for the memories to take me away again.

Chapter Seven

The next morning I'm so hungover, I can barely get out of bed. Thank God Blaze slept over, because we both ended up needing a buddy to hold each other's hair back as the contents of last night's vodka resurfaced into my mom's heated porcelain toilet.

After I had gone back to sleep, I didn't have any more dreams—at least, none that I can remember. It's sad, but the current pounding in my head makes it hard to think about anything else at the moment.

"I feel," Blaze moans on the bathroom floor, "like absolute trash."

"You and me both. What kind of vodka did we drink last night?"

Blaze gives me a look and I can't tell if it's one that says "do you really care?" or "how should I know?" The answer to either is hilarious. We both erupt into a fit of laughter and then reluctantly hold onto our stomachs at the pain. Laughing after puking, not the best idea.

"I think I want Chinese food." I look up at her.

"Alex, it's 11:00 in the morning."

"So? Chinese restaurants are always open. Watch," I say and pull out my phone, already dialing the China Wok contact card. Of course I have it saved, it's my favorite cuisine of all time. Next to chocolate chip pancakes of course.

"Hi, yes... can I get a large order of sweet and sour chicken, extra rice, a small Lo Mein, and a side of egg rolls." I wink at Blaze as I say the order.

"How many?" I repeat the cashier's question. "Hmm, let's do six. Great, thank you!" I give them my name and address and hang up the phone, smiling widely at Blaze.

"See, I told you they were open. Even on Christmas Day, you can always count on getting Chinese food."

"Okay, great but, did you really need to order *six* egg rolls?"

"What, do you think I should call them back and make it ten?"

I'm being totally serious—I love my egg rolls, but Blaze erupts into another fit of laughter at what she thinks is a joke. I join in, clutching my stomach and already drooling over the meal that's on its way. I don't care what anyone says, Chinese food is the best hangover cure of all time.

When our food arrives, we pile it onto the coffee table in the living room and turn on Netflix. We've been binge watching *Inventing Anna* this past week, and we're on the last episode. I can't wait to find out what happens in the trial of the fake German heiress.

Blaze and I spend most of the day on the couch, and despite me trying to convince her to stay the night again, she heads home shortly after dinner, which turned out to be reheated Chinese food from earlier. I know I will see her tomorrow at school, but once she leaves, the house suddenly feels much bigger than it was before.

My mom is still at work, texted that she was stuck with a client. There's no way I'm going to call Jenna for company, our last conversation still leaving residual anger deep in my gut.

I'm on my own.

I grab another egg roll out of the fridge, not even bothering to heat it up, and plop back down on the couch to find something else to watch. The house is quiet, and it's almost as if I can hear every single breath that I take. I jump and turn around a few times at noises I think I hear, but settle back into the couch when I realize there's no one else here.

Only me. With my thoughts and memories to keep me company.

I really hate being alone.

****

The following Monday at school is like any other. Classes, lunch, more classes. I haven't heard from Jordan all weekend, and I'm beyond pissed at this point. He sits down next to me at the lunch table now, hoping to take a bite of his French fry, but not knowing that I need him to use his mouth for something else.

"Where the hell were you all weekend?"

He reflexively pulls away from me as if he suddenly notices I'm sitting here. This only pisses me off more. I drag his tray of French fries completely out from his reach.

"Lexie, babe, I'm sorry I—I got tied up," he laughs at me. I notice Paige blush out of the corner of my eye. *What the hell?* My anger at Paige never dissipated, even after her fake apology at Daniel's party. My eyes have no desire to pay her any attention today.

Instead, they look back at Jordan, who's staring at me like he's waiting for *me* to answer *him*. I have no idea what he wants me to say. He's the one who owes me an explanation, not the other way around.

I cross my arms and raise one eyebrow at him. I love this trick, it took me years to perfect and I've always wanted the opportunity to use it. Being able to do it on Jordan now makes it that much better.

"I'm sorry, really. But clearly you got home safe on Friday, and I heard you and Blaze had fun at Daniel's." He reaches for the tray of fries. I let him take it.

"We did, but I would have had more fun if you were there," I say to him. "I missed you."

He leans over and kisses my cheek, leaving a sticky residue of salt and fried potatoes from where his lips meet my skin. I wipe off the crumbs and wait for him to tell me what happened, where he really was all weekend. I wait for him to say he missed me too. But he doesn't.

I feel defeated, and clearly am not going to get anywhere with him. Maybe something happened with his family, something personal that he doesn't want to talk about in front of everyone. I'm hoping he will tell me later.

"So which house are we hitting this weekend?" he directs his attention back to the rest of the group.

He's acting like everything is fine. Like it's totally normal that he didn't see his girlfriend over the weekend. And that it doesn't even matter that he didn't bother to call or text her, letting her know he was okay.

Paige is staring at me now and at first, I think I catch a glimpse of sympathy in her eyes. But when she shrugs her shoulders and casually grabs one of Jordan's fries off his tray, I see him winking at her. Something tightens in my stomach at the sight, but I try not to let it take over.

An angry girlfriend is one thing, but a jealous one is a whole other ballgame. My feelings aside, I turn back to the group at the table and try to focus on a conversation to join.

"You all are going to die when you see my dress," Paige says to the guys.

"I bet it looks even better off than it does on." One of the guys, Jake, I think, winks at her. Gross.

This weekend is Homecoming, and I have been so excited to be Jordan's date. He never actually asked me to go with him, not in the cute promposal way other boyfriends were asking their dates, but I still know we're going together. And that's still the case, despite him being MIA this past weekend. Right?

For a moment, worries of him breaking up with me take over my thoughts. Wondering if that's why he was nowhere to be found this weekend, if that's where he was—off somewhere planning it out, what to say to me, where to do it, what time of day would be best.

My anxiety is getting the best of me now. My thoughts need to be reset.

If Jordan wants to break up with me, he would have done it by now. He wouldn't have waited all weekend, and he certainly wouldn't have missed out on two parties because he was planning the perfect break up. He probably would've sent me a text. I know Jordan pretty well, and he's definitely the type of guy who would break up with someone over text.

I don't know how to feel about the way the thought reassures me. Shouldn't I want to be with someone who *didn't* break up with a girl over text?

Another thought enters my mind. *What if he's waiting to do it at the dance? No*, I think. There's no way he would pull a *Carrie* on me. Jordan isn't like that. At least I don't think he's like that.

This isn't working. Full on crazy is commencing in the back of my mind. I need to let it go. It's going to be a long week at school, and if Jordan is going to break up with me, I'm sure he isn't going to do it the week of homecoming. It means too much to him. It means too much to *me*, I realize.

"I need to pee. Lex, want to come with?" Paige asks me. I don't need to pee, and I don't really want to go with her, but something about her tone convinces me to get up and go to the bathroom with her. Maybe she's going to give me a real apology this time.

Becca stands up to follow, and I realize she's been

sitting at the lunch table this whole time. *Huh*, I think. I didn't even notice her.

"No, Bex. Just Lex." Paige chuckles at her use of the rhyme and motions me to follow her out of the cafeteria.

There are bathrooms inside the lunch area, but none of us ever dare to use them. They're always gross and smell horrible. Not that any bathroom is necessarily clean in our school, but these are definitely the worst.

We walk around the cafeteria and down the art hallway, finally reaching our destination. Paige is silent the entire walk, stepping two paces in front of me the whole time, almost as if she doesn't want to be seen with me.

Once inside the bathroom, she briefly bends down to check that each stall is empty. They are, so she comes over to face me and grabs my hands. The anxiety I felt at the lunch table is multiplied now and I want her to get on with it. Whatever *it* is.

"Look, I don't know how to bring this up so I'm going to come right out and say it." She takes a breath.

Oh, no. Whatever she's about to say is not going to be good. I close my eyes and try to prepare myself for the worst, although I'm not even sure what that could be at this moment. I'm still mad at her from what she said at the diner, and her lame attempt at an apology at Daniel's party. I really have no idea what's going to come out of her mouth now.

"You need to have sex with Jordan," I hear her say quickly.

My eyes open so fast they probably could pop right out of my head. Whatever I was expecting her to say, this was definitely not it. For a moment, I wonder if I imagined the words that came out of her mouth. But the frown on her face is such a mix of sadness and disgust that I know I heard her correctly.

"Excuse me?"

"I know you're a virgin, and that's super sweet and all, but you're going to lose him if you don't do something."

Is she serious? Who does this girl think she is, dragging me away from the lunch table to tell me I need to sleep with my boyfriend. He's *my* boyfriend, not hers. I think I would know if he isn't happy with how our relationship is going.

My almost panic attack at the lunch table resurges, the crazy thoughts about Jordan breaking up with me entering my brain once again. The last thing Paige needs to know is that I'm having doubts about him. Knowing her, she would spread any uncertainty I shared around the school like wildfire, using any and all information she could to get rid of me.

Confidence is what I need now. She cannot see me crack. This is the second time she's bringing up my sex life with my boyfriend and I'm over it.

"One, this is none of your business. Two, I'm not having sex with Jordan to keep being his girlfriend. He knows that, and he doesn't expect anything."

The look she gives me next makes me question everything about my statement.

"Does he?" I ask her.

"I've known Jordan for a long time," she says and again, gives me that sad smile that morphs into a frown.

"I have watched him have many girlfriends, and none typically last more than a few months. He's a player, yes, but he's a player with needs." My stomach lurches at the way she says *needs*. I think I'm going to be sick.

Jordan and I have a pretty PG relationship, and it's working fine. At least, I thought it was. Not accounting for my whole *he's going to break up with me* at the lunch table dilemma. We have only been dating for a few months, does he really expect me to sleep with him by now? If that's true, maybe I don't know Jordan as well as I thought I did. *Maybe I don't want to.*

But what if Paige is messing with me, trying to get under my skin? What if this is another one of her games, like her outburst at the diner. She can't be trusted and she definitely doesn't have my best interest at heart. So why is she trying to help me now?

"This weekend is big for him, with the game and the dance and all that. He looks forward to homecoming events all year long. And the celebrations after even more so." She winks at me.

Violation and disgust fill my body from her wink. This is all making me feel horribly wrong. No, she has to be joking. I'm sure of it.

"Paige, I am not losing my virginity on homecoming night."

Despite the cliche, I can't even process something so monumental happening because it's Jordan's most popular night of the year. My stomach lurches and the temptation to dive headfirst into a bathroom stall surges through me.

Paige keeps staring at me, like she's still holding back what she really wants to say. *You have got to be kidding me.*

"Is there more?" I ask. *I don't really want to know.*

She doesn't answer me, but I can tell she's considering her words carefully. *Nope, I definitely don't want to know.*

"I really don't know if it's my place to say," she says and walks over to where the sinks are, pulling out a tube of lipstick from her pocket.

She keeps me waiting, and applies a coat of matte pink color to her mouth. I keep waiting for her to continue, but she doesn't. Her dramatic antics are really starting to get under my skin.

What could be so bad that she couldn't tell me? She already came right out and said I need to lose my virginity to my boyfriend. It can't get much worse than that.

Unless it can.

Because maybe what she doesn't want to say is what I have been thinking all along. It's what I've worried about all weekend, and have been too scared to say out loud. Looking at Paige now, understanding this conversation, I realize there might be more truth to my fears than I think. And I need to know for sure.

"He's going to dump me if I don't sleep with him, isn't he?" I ask her.

The way she looks briefly to the ground and avoids my eyes is the answer in and of itself.

"I'm not trying to pressure you, I just thought you should know." She places her hand on my arm and gives me a sad smile before walking out of the restroom.

Great. Even though Paige pisses me off, she has a point. The truth of that fact makes me dislike her even more than I already do.

Jordan isn't going to keep dating me if all we do together is kiss. A part of me knew that even when he first asked me out, but I thought we would deal with it when the situation came about. I thought it would be *months*, maybe even a year down the road before we would talk about it. I didn't think it would happen this fast.

And what if Paige is lying? What if she told me all of this to send me spiraling, and then I practically throw myself at Jordan, when none of this is true, making a fool out of myself?

That's exactly what Paige wants. To send me packing while everyone else has a good laugh. She's so untrustworthy, there's no way for me to know if any of her words are the truth.

Only one person can validate them. I need to talk to Jordan.

My brain is overwhelmed, thoughts and emotions from the past few days getting the better of me. A few tears have fallen down my face, which I frantically wipe away. The bathroom sink squeaks as I turn the faucet, cold water splashing onto my cheeks before my reflection in the mirror catches my eye.

My face is a little puffy, and dark circles are starting to form underneath my eyes. Despite my best efforts getting ready this morning, I couldn't seem to get rid of them. Oh well. *I've looked worse*, I think to myself.

My eyes close as a deep breath flows in and out of my nose, opening again when I push through the bathroom door to head back to the lunch table.

Smack! The door ricochets back into my face and I'm on the ground.

Pain enters my skull and my vision darkens. Something clatters to the floor, sounding like a pile of books on the tile hallway.

"Shit, I'm so sorry—oh, hey, Alex," a vaguely familiar voice says.

The black dots that took over my vision start to fade the more I blink, and a figure comes into focus in front of me. He's holding out a hand and looking at me expectantly, those emerald eyes piercing into my soul.

"You have got to be kidding me," I say to Cameron, ignoring his hand and pushing myself up from the floor.

"Oh, come on, it was an accident. How was I

supposed to know you were going to walk out of the bathroom at the exact moment I was going to walk by it?"

I scoff at him and try to walk past him when he grabs my arm and turns me back around. An electric current *zings* throughout my body. I rip my arm out from his grip quickly.

"What do you want?" I stare at him.

"I—" he stops short. "Nothing, but… are you okay? You look upset."

"Upset?" I laugh. "Of course I'm upset! I'm standing here talking to you instead of having lunch with my boyfriend. You know, the star quarterback of the football team? The one you claim you have no idea exists? Well he does, and you are preventing me from being with him right now."

"I don't know what game you are trying to play here but this," I gesture at the space between him and me. "Is not going to happen. So why don't you do both of us a favor and leave me alone."

I start to walk away when I hear what sounds like clapping behind me. *Is he serious?* I spin back around to face him, much angrier than I was a moment ago. Today is not a good day to mess with me.

"Bravo, that was really something." He continues to clap at me before he bends down to pick up the fallen books, his laugh fresh in my ears.

"What are you talking about?" I question him.

"That little performance. You playing the mean girl. You did it well, too. I almost believed you."

"Excuse me?"

"Oh, come on, Alex, this isn't who you are. I would expect this attitude from Paige, sure. Maybe even Becca. But not from you."

I open my mouth in pure shock at the audacity of

this guy. He doesn't even know me, and here he is accusing me of putting on a—what did he say? A *performance*. I want to pick up the books he dropped so I could throw them at his perfect looking face.

"Listen to me," I point my finger at him. "I don't know who you think you are and honestly, I don't really care. I don't know why the concept of listening seems new to you, but if you are going to believe anything I say, believe this. You are really starting to piss me off. Stop following me." I turn on my heel and storm off, heading back into the cafeteria. I don't even stop when I hear the faintest of chuckles coming from behind me. *The nerve.*

Back at the table my rage is fuming. Jordan is still sitting there, chatting with the football boys about some sort of play or move they want to make during the game on Friday. I lean over his shoulder and gently kiss his cheek, more for myself than for him. He swats me away like I've annoyed him, so I sit back down and pick at his fries, which are now cold on his lunch tray.

I watch as he smiles and laughs with the guys and I stare as he plays around flirtatiously with the girls. He doesn't even give me a second look. It's like I'm not even there. I glance over at Paige who shrugs as if to say, "I told you so," and sink further into my seat.

My anger from interacting with Cam and anxiety over my conversation with Paige is playing all over my face. I have no idea what's going on. But I do know one thing now—Paige was telling the truth. It wasn't some game, some way to play a prank on me and oust me from the popular table. She was being completely serious in the bathroom.

If I don't do something, I am going to lose my boyfriend. The thought alone stirs something inside of me, but I can't quite put my finger on it.

I don't want Jordan to dump me, but I don't know

if I'm ready to do what he's asking me to do either—not that he's the one asking, more like expecting. And I really don't want to give Cameron any more reason to have something over me. Mostly, I really don't want Paige to be right. I hate when she's right.

****

As the rest of the school week goes by, I'm barely there.

Physically, I go to my classes and do my best to pay attention. I take notes, even though I don't understand half of what I'm writing down. I sit at the lunch table with the group. I laugh when someone tells a joke, even if I don't think it's funny. I hold Jordan's hand in the hallway, and I kiss him goodbye at the end of every day. I do my best at soccer practice. I listen to my coach and perform all the drills he instructs to the best of my ability. I ride to and from school with Blaze, listening to the radio and singing along to whatever song is playing.

Mentally, I'm anywhere else. I can't stop thinking about the homecoming dance and what the rest of the night will bring for me.

I have no idea what to do. And I'm running out of time.

ANDIE L. SMITH

Chapter Eight

"And the extra point is good!" The announcer screams into the microphone.

I jump to my feet for what feels like the fifteenth time this evening, cheering Jordan on at the homecoming game—the biggest game of the year for our school. We're playing our rival, the Lake City Bengals, and the score is 17-14. Our team is in the lead, but with over five minutes left in the fourth quarter, there's still plenty of time left for the other team to take the win out from under us.

Football is one of my favorite sports, next to soccer. Once I started playing, my dad introduced me to so many other sports—football, baseball, even hockey. I ate them all up. Sunday RedZone days with my dad were the best. Without saying it, I knew it made him happy that he could share sports with me. He probably wanted a son, but he got Jenna and me instead.

After I became interested, I think he was okay with the result. Jenna never cared about sports. She always ran off with my mom somewhere during the Super Bowl or the Stanley Cup Final. But not me. If there was a game on, my dad and I would be watching it together.

Now I'm standing in the bleachers and cheering on my quarterback boyfriend. If only my dad could see me like this. I wonder what he would say about me dating Jordan. He probably would have loved him, if only for the chance to talk about football nonstop with someone that wasn't me. The son he never got.

A breeze blows over the stands and I tighten my jean jacket around me. The weather has been doing this weird flip-flop between cold and hot each day, which makes it hard to dress properly. Luckily, I'm wearing jeans, but that's mainly because of the bonfire party after the game.

"Go Jordan!" I hear a scream come from a few rows lower than me.

Jordan runs off the field to the sidelines, the other team's offense taking over. At the sound of his name, he looks over to the direction the voice is coming from. My eyes follow his gaze and notice who called out the cheer for my boyfriend.

Standing on the sidelines, in her blue and gold cheerleading uniform is Paige. The uniform is pretty standard for cheerleaders—a very short skirt and a halter tank top that cuts off under her rib cage. It looks cute on her, as does everything. *She must be freezing*.

Paige is shaking her shiny blue and gold pom poms together——our school colors—and kicking her leg up in the air. I flinch at the movement and briefly wonder how someone could be that flexible without hurting themselves. If it were me, I would have probably found a way to break some important bone.

"They're really good friends, you know," Becca says next to me.

Even though she had no idea what was going on during the game, I'm glad Becca came with me. I hate coming to games alone.

After a few drives, she asked me to explain what being offside meant. I tried to draw it out for her, but had to give up when I lost her at a discussion over the line of scrimmage. She asked me to let her know when we scored or did something big that required her to jump up and down in celebration. *Easy enough*.

"What are you talking about?" I question her now. I had no idea what she meant.

"Jordan and Paige. I know sometimes it seems

like they're flirting, but they're not. They've known each other practically since birth, so they're really good friends."

I wasn't even thinking about Jordan and Paige flirting until she brought it up. Now that she has, it's all I can think about.

Am I missing something? I try to think over the last couple of weeks for any times Jordan and Paige interacted in a weird way. But they're always being weird and I can't pinpoint their flirting over Paige being, well, Paige.

My skin suddenly feels flushed and my chest tightens as if my clothes are practically glued to my skin. The confusing thoughts and close proximity with all the other students is not doing me any good.

Space. I need space. I need to breathe.

"I'm going to go get another drink," I say to Becca. "Do you want anything?"

She shakes her head at me and looks back to the field, confusion forming in her brows. I already know she's not going to have any idea about what's happening without me standing next to her. My break needs to be quick.

My frustration grows when I see the long line at the concession stand. A groan escapes my lips, a headache already forming in the back of my mind from lack of caffeine. The stand is all the way across the field in the opposing team's end zone, so I can't quite see where the game is now that our team has the ball back.

After paying for my Diet Coke, I put my change in the tip bar on the counter for the rest of the students working the shift tonight. I start to head back to the bleachers, hoping to save Becca from losing another brain cell, when something catches my eye—or rather, someone.

He's standing by the goal post, his arms draped over the fence that lines the outskirts of the field. His dark jeans and black leather jacket are all I can see from here. *That stupid jacket.*

There really is no reason for me to go over to him. I don't have anything to say to him, and I know the moment he opens his mouth I will feel annoyed. My mind is yelling at me to go back to the stands, to watch my boyfriend finish one of the biggest games of the season and explain to Becca what a touchdown is for the hundredth time this evening.

But something pushes my feet forward, in the opposite direction of the bleachers.

Towards him.

"Not really your scene, huh?" I call out.

Cameron turns around so quickly, he trips over his feet and almost falls to the ground. He catches himself on the chain-link fence and stands up straight, as if trying to cover up the way he almost completely busted it in front of me. A small laugh escapes me. What a dork. But at least he's a cute dork. *Wait, what?*

"What are you doing here?" he asks me.

"Are you serious?" I glance over to the field, where our team is now in the end zone on the opposite side, Jordan in position in the center.

"Oh, right. The quarterback." He shakes his head.

"Did you think I was lying?"

"No, I knew you were telling the truth." He stares at me and I walk over to stand next to him against the fence.

"So if all this," I wave around in the direction of the field, "is not your scene, then what are *you* doing here?"

"Okay, you caught me."

I can't help it, his response intrigues me. My

eyebrow raises and my lips part in interest.

"You're right, I am following you. I don't know why, but I can't get you out of my head." He turns to face me.

My chest tightens and a small gasp escapes. I think he hears it.

Our faces are hovering so close together, I can see the freckles that hide shyly under his wavy tendrils at the top of his forehead. My eyes betray me, and I reflexively glance down at his lips, which look so full and so close to my own that my breath hitches in my throat. My heart is beating so fast, the throbbing sound so loud it's making my headache worse. I'm sure he could hear that too.

He presses his body a little closer to mine and I lean my head in ever so slightly… when he dramatically places a hand across his chest and takes a giant step back.

"Oh, Alexandra, please put me out of my misery and say you'll be mine!"

I shrink backwards and blink a few times to truly understand what happened. What was about to happen.

Cameron's laughing at me now, his upper body leaning over his legs and his face looking up to mine with tears in his eyes. In an instant, my heart plummets to the floor and my stomach feels sour.

The sudden rush of screams and chants directs my attention back to the field. The crowd in the stands are all on their feet, jumping up and down with their arms in the air. Our offensive line is rushing into the endzone, tackling my boyfriend in a hug before lifting him up on their shoulders and prancing him around the field.

Jordan threw the game winning touchdown. And I missed it.

Because I'm over here, on the complete opposite side of the field, entertaining some Justin Bieber wannabe instead of standing in the bleachers with the rest of my peers, cheering on the person who is supposed to be the only guy in my life. The embarrassment makes me angry and I feel so stupid for walking over here in the first place.

"You're pathetic," I say to Cameron. He's still laughing.

I storm off and head back towards the bleachers, where I wait for Becca to walk down and find me so we can drive over to the bonfire together. I know she probably has a million questions about that last play, and I'm not sure I'm even going to be able to answer them.

My pulse is racing, my heart beating so fast, stars begin to cloud my vision. If it wasn't for Becca's grip on my arm, I'm sure I would collapse right here in the parking lot.

I don't know what's more confusing. The fact that I thought Cameron was about to kiss me, or how much I really wanted him to.

****

"I am *alive!*" Becca shouts from the roof of her mom's convertible. She brings her head back inside the vehicle and I'm laughing hysterically in the backseat.

Her actions send me to another time, another place entirely.

It was freshman year, and we were on the way home from my soccer game. I was sitting in the front seat of my dad's convertible as he drove. Mom never let me sit in the front seat, but Dad always did.

The windows were down but the top was still on. It was early September, so the West Virginia weather was a perfect blend of sunny, but breezy and cool at the same time. I had my head out the window, enjoying the fresh air on my face as we drove.

My dad pulled over to the side of the road and I glanced at him, wondering what was wrong. He held up his hand, his usual way of telling me to wait. He smiled, and out of nowhere I was met with the familiar sound of machinery coming from the back of the car. I watched as the top of the convertible removed itself and folded back into the trunk of the car.

My hands shot straight up to the sky and a joyful scream escaped the back of my throat as he pulled back onto the highway. Driving with the top down was almost as fun as going to the beach. And my dad knew how much I loved the beach.

We turned the radio up as a Rascal Flatts song beamed throughout the car. Country music wasn't really my thing, but this band was special to me and my dad. So much so that he took me to see them live when I was fourteen, my first ever concert. A night I will never forget.

We drove home the long way, singing and dancing in the open air like it was the only thing we had to do that day.

I remember sitting there thinking if life could be like this forever, I would be so happy.

That's how life always was with my dad—fun and free. And I missed it. God, I missed it, and him, so much. But I could never say that out loud. I was the only one who felt that way.

"Whoa, Lex, you have to try that! It's exhilarating!" Becca screams at me as Blaze leans over to pull her back into her seat.

It takes me a minute to realize I'm in the backseat of Becca's convertible and not my dad's car. In my moment of confusion, she reaches over and grabs the flask from my hand, taking a huge sip in the process.

"Hey, that's mine! I told you to bring your own." I shake my head at her.

Paige is driving, and she hasn't been drinking yet.

But there's no way in hell I'm standing up and sticking my head out of the sunroof.

Looking over at Paige, I notice she's still in her cheerleading uniform, not bothering to change after the game. I guess I can't blame her. If I looked like her, I probably wouldn't want to change out of the revealing outfit either.

"So, little Lexie, are you ready to become a woman tomorrow night?" Paige winks at me from the rearview mirror.

"What is she talking about?" Blaze looks at me incredulously.

We picked up Blaze on the way. She didn't want to come to the game, but as always, is down for a good bonfire party. I'm glad, because I don't know if I can be around Paige without having my best friend near me.

Ever since that day in the bathroom, I have been avoiding Paige and saying as little as possible to her at the lunch table. She needs to think that I'm handling it. There can't be any reason for her to doubt me. Especially after what Becca said at the game, about Paige and Jordan always flirting. It makes me wonder if there's some other ulterior motive Paige has for pulling the rug out from under me. If somehow, she's taking matters into her own hands.

I feel my cheeks redden and shoot Paige a glare through the mirror.

"She's joking, and it is *not* funny," I say, throwing my words at Paige while shrugging at Blaze in response.

With the flask back in my hands, I take a long sip, wincing as the alcohol burns going down my throat. I still haven't decided what I'm going to do about Jordan and the big V-card situation. But Paige doesn't need to know that. And Blaze definitely doesn't either.

We pull up to Timothy Harrison's house, and I'm

thankful for the distraction of drunk guys and girls wearing little to no clothing as we get out of the car. Timothy was our school's football quarterback a few years ago, until Jordan came along and outranked all of his titles and records. His parents aren't as rich as some of the other kids in our school, but they own a lot of land that's been passed down through the family. His one-story brick house isn't much to see on the outside, but the backyard stretches on for miles. It's the perfect spot for a bonfire, and Timothy loves to burn things. Especially during homecoming weekend.

As soon as we walk to the middle of the open field, Becca runs off with her phone glued to her face. Her boyfriend Daniel is away for the weekend, skiing with his family in Colorado. Becca is furious he ditched her on Homecoming and she's paranoid that he's going to find some sort of "snow bunny" (her words) and cheat on her. He probably will, but Becca hasn't always been too faithful either, so I'm not sure why she picked tonight to change things up.

I turn to Paige, but find myself staring at empty space. The sound of her laugh comes from off in the distance and I turn, spotting her a few feet away. She already has a drink in her hand and a boy on her arm. Paige knows how to work a room and obviously understood the meaning of "there is no time to waste."

Again, in that outfit, I probably would've done the same thing. Probably.

Blaze and I share a look and laugh as we walk toward the flames and find a stack of red cups next to some kegs. After pouring myself a drink, I'm engulfed by two strong, warm arms wrapping around my waist.

"Come with me," Jordan's lips are against my ear as he whispers to me.

His touch sends a shiver down my spine and I

grab his hand, waving to Blaze and following him towards the back of the woods.

"Jordan, you better not be taking me out here to chop me up with a chainsaw." He laughs at me and pulls me further into the woods, stopping at a little clearing in between a few trees.

"I'm serious," I say. "This better not be a live action role play of one of your horror movies."

I try to adjust my eyes to the darkness of the forest and take in what I see in front of me. There's a red blanket spread out on the ground and a six pack of beer lying on one of the corners. A flashlight turns on from next to me, and Jordan holds his phone up so he can make his way over to the blanket.

"For us, my lady," Jordan slurs and winks at me before sitting down on the blanket and tapping the space next to him.

We had come from the football game, but I have no idea how he's already drunk this quickly. I try to remember how big of a deal this weekend is for him and nestle into his side on the blanket. He did win the game after all, he deserves to let loose tonight.

"Congrats on the win," I say to him.

My mind goes back to the moment and how I completely missed his winning touchdown because I was almost locking my lips with another guy—a guy who I absolutely could not stand. Jordan doesn't need to know that.

"Thanks, babe. But we can do something a little more personal to celebrate." He smiles lazily at me and my chest tightens.

He leans over and kisses me intensely. I almost forget we're in the middle of the woods as I lose myself in his mouth. His hands are everywhere. In my hair, on my arms, sliding down my back. Until they reach around the front of my waist and start unbuttoning my jeans.

"Jordan—" I try to say in between his kisses.

He doesn't hear me, or if he does, he acts like he doesn't. His hands break the button of my jeans free, but instead of moving on to the zipper, he slides them underneath my shirt and starts to graze the outside of my bra.

This is not happening. Not now. I'm not ready for this. I thought I had more time.

"Jordan, stop!" I break free from his mouth and push against his chest.

Is he seriously trying to have sex with me right now? In the middle of the woods, at a bonfire where anyone could walk in on us doing it.

He groans and rolls his eyes at me but removes his hands from my body. I notice how quickly the warmth from his touch turns to ice against my skin. He lays down on the blanket and throws his arm over his face, as if he's blocking out the sun... but it's pitch black under the night sky.

"I-I'm sorry," I stutter. I know I've upset him and that's the last thing I want to do.

"Are you?" His question shocks me.

I expected him to tell me it was fine, that we can wait as long as I need to. A part of me is still hoping that Paige is wrong, that my relationship with Jordan isn't on the line. That he's better than this.

"What?" I furrow my brow in confusion.

"Are you sorry? Because we've been going out for months now, and you won't even let me get to second base. Do you know how that makes me look?"

My mouth drops open and I can't seem to form any words. Suddenly, I know that any part of me still holding out hope for us is completely wrong. At least he isn't done talking, which saves me from having to say anything at all. Not that I know what I was going to say in the first place.

"Look, I still like you. But a guy like me has needs, and I have a reputation to uphold."

I flinch at the word *needs* and remember Paige saying the exact same thing. The thought brings me back to the conversation I had with her in the bathroom a few days ago. And what she said would happen if I didn't 'do something' about it.

Ugh. The last thing I want is for Paige Garrison to be right. A small part of me was still hoping she was joking. But as the scene plays out in front of me, I know she was telling the truth.

"Are you breaking up with me?" I feel the tears start to swell in my eyes.

He's quiet for a minute too long and a pit forms in my stomach. This is it. This is really happening. I try to take a deep breath and not let any tears fall. If this is the end, I'm not going to let him see me cry.

He blows out a breath and I close my eyes, preparing myself for what he's going to say next.

"The dance is tomorrow, I would look like an asshole if I dumped you before it," he sighs and grabs my hand, playing with my fingers. I used to love it when he did that. Now it felt fake. Like he isn't doing it because he wants to. He's doing it because he has to.

Even though it's not exactly what I'm expecting him to say, his response still makes me angry. The only reason he isn't breaking up with me right now is to save face, to keep his precious reputation intact. I don't know whether to slap him in the face at this or be somewhat grateful he also isn't going to make a fool out of me during homecoming weekend.

"I don't want to break up, and we don't have to. Not if we can start doing, you know, stuff," he adds.

My breath catches in my throat and I can physically feel my heart drop into my stomach. Everything Paige said was the truth. Jordan is going to dump me if I don't give him something he *needs*. Am I making it a bigger deal than it is? Does losing my virginity really matter in the grand scheme of things, when if I don't do it I'll lose Jordan instead?

If I did lose him, would that be so bad?

I try to think about what my life would look like if Jordan and I broke up and it's hard. My spot at the lunch table would be revoked and I doubt Paige or Becca would still want to be my friend.

Blaze would stick by me, of course, but that would be it.

Jordan wouldn't come to my soccer games anymore, and who knows what that would do to the turnout and motivation for the team. The party invitations would probably end, and I really love going to the parties. Being at them, being with Jordan, it helps me not think about my dad. It helps me get over it, as everyone keeps pushing me to do.

I'm not ready to face the idea of what living without that would be like. Not yet. At that understanding, the decision is easy.

"Okay," I say to Jordan and hold his hand in mine. "I understand, and I want to be with you. All the way. Why don't we do it after the dance tomorrow?" The words taste sour on my tongue.

The sinking feeling in my gut is so surreal I can physically feel a weight pulling my body down. My breath deepens and I try to plaster on what I hope is a convincing smile. Jordan's face brightens almost immediately and he leans in to kiss me urgently once more.

"I knew you were cool, babe," he says and leans

back to crack open two of the beers from the six pack sitting on the blanket.

As he hands me a can, the sinking feeling in my stomach grows but I lean my head back to take a huge sip, hoping to wash it away with the acidic bitterness of the beer. *Cool?*

"Can we go back to the bonfire now?" I ask him.

Even though I know he isn't going to try anything again tonight, I still feel weird being alone with him. There's also a strong possibility that if I continue to sit here with him like this, I'm going to change my mind.

"Sure, babe."

We walk back out to the open field and I reach for Jordan's hand, but he's no longer next me. I look around and see that he's already halfway across the field, chugging down his can of beer and slapping the rest of the football guys on the shoulder. We had made plans to sleep together, and yet he can't seem to get away from me fast enough.

Maybe he wants to share the good news with his friends, I think.

I shouldn't let his absence bother me so much. He's Jordan Tucker after all. I'm not the only one who wants his company. *Be cool, Lex.*

But I'm anything but cool. Somehow, I'm always the one missing out. I walk back over to Blaze, still standing right next to the fire where I left her.

"Everything okay?" she asks me.

A small part of me wants to scream "No! Absolutely nothing is okay!" but I know better. Once again, I suppress the urge to say what I really want to say. To acknowledge how I really feel.

"Yep. Everything's fine," I plaster the same fake smile I gave to Jordan on my face and grab another can of beer, pulling Blaze into the depths of fire, ready to burn the rest of the night away.

****

"So are you excited about the dance tonight?" my mom asks me as I continue to rub lotion on my freshly shaven legs.

There are so many answers to her question. No, yes, I don't know, not really. I have no idea which one is the truth. Because of course I'm excited to dress up and dance with my boyfriend and best friends. It's what I promised to do after the dance that has me questioning everything.

"You know it!" I beam at my mom, hoping she doesn't catch the shakiness in my voice.

Once my legs are done, I walk over and sit at the vanity in my mom's bathroom. It's huge, twice the size of one you would see in the presidential suite in a fancy hotel. This has always been my favorite place to get ready.

My mom comes over and starts to curl my hair, only lightly to still allow for my natural waves. I glance over at the clock and breathe a sigh of relief that I still have about three hours before Jordan gets here. Time was ticking. Quite literally.

"You look so beautiful," she says to me.

"I haven't even put on my makeup yet." I laugh at her.

"Doesn't matter," she shakes her slightly. "You are naturally gorgeous. Your dad would be so proud." My chest tightens at her words and the sinking feeling returns to my stomach.

"We never talk about him," I say.

"What do you mean?"

"Dad. We never talk about his death, or anything about when he was alive."

"What's there to talk about, dear?" Her question

sends a fresh shot of pain deep into my gut.

What's there to talk about? Oh, I don't know, *everything*? How about the fact that my dad died, for one. He's no longer walking this earth and I will never see him again. Or for two, that my dreams are filled with memories of when he was alive, but there is no one to share those with. The fact that not only his death doesn't matter, but apparently his life doesn't either.

But again, I'm the only one bothered by all of this. I'm the only one going partially insane.

"Never mind." I shrug her off and glance at the clock again. "When is Jenna going to get here?"

She had promised she would come home for the weekend to help me get ready, but it's getting closer and closer to when I need to be heading out and she isn't here yet. I should've known better than to have believed her. She hasn't been back home ever since the night we found out Dad died.

"Oh, Alex, she was too busy with mid-terms and said to send her your pictures. I thought she told you," my mom says quickly. I could tell by her tone what she really means is that my sister has no desire to come.

I'd be lying if I say I'm not a little bit hurt. My sister has always been my favorite person in the entire world. She's two years older than me and I have always looked up to her. When we were little, I would follow her around everywhere. She got annoyed with me a lot of the time, but I didn't care. I always wanted to be near her.

Things would be different next year, I would be applying to colleges and getting ready to move out, and who knows where I was going to end up. She stayed close to home and is going to West Virginia University, which is only about two hours away from Summersville.

I remember when she got in, I was so excited to still have her so close and she promised she would come home all the time. Which she did, until Dad died. It's like he disappeared and he took Jenna with him. We barely talk anymore, and I miss her so much. Seeing as she couldn't bother to come help me get ready tonight, I don't think I can say she feels the same way about me. Thinking about her makes my heart swell, even though it hurts at the same time from how she pushed me away so easily when I asked her to visit Dad with me. I try to remember the last conversation we had. It was only a few weeks ago, and I called her to see how she was doing. She had finished telling me about the sorority she was joining, Alpha Zeta Pi or something like that. The phone call plays back in my head as I try to remember if I missed anything.

"Oh, my gosh, Alex, there is the cutest girl rushing with me," she said.

"Rushing? Like she's pressuring you?" I cluelessly asked her.

"No stupid, rushing the sorority. It's what they call new sisters looking to join," she laughed as if it was so obvious. "I swear, sometimes you can be such a tomboy."

"Just because I like to play soccer and don't know sorority terms doesn't mean I'm a tomboy." I poked at her, but still felt hurt by her words.

"Whatever, I'll make sure you look as girly as possible when I help you get ready for the dance," she promised.

"I'm so excited! I can't wait for Jordan to see my dress."

"You guys are so cute together. I can't wait to finally meet the boy who makes my little sister all mushy gushy," Jenna laughed.

"I think you'll really like him. Dad would have, too."

She was quiet and I thought for a moment the call failed. I brought the phone away from my face and checked, but it was still on our call, the minutes counting up and Jenna's name still reflected at the top of the screen.

"Jenna? Are you there?" I asked.

"I'm here."

Oh. Maybe she was thinking about Dad. About time.

"I wish Dad could see me in my dress," I continued.

"Alex, stop." Her sharp tone caught me off guard.

"What?"

"Don't bring him up. You know I don't like talking about him," she snapped.

I reflexively took a step back in my room, even though she couldn't see that.

This was always happening with Jenna. Any time I brought up something about Dad, whether that be a memory or a new opportunity I wished he was here for, she immediately shut me down. She got so angry, like I had no business bringing him up in the first place. It confused the hell out of me.

"All I said was I wish he could've seen me in my homecoming dress," I practically whispered, my tone soft.

"Yeah, well, there's no point in saying that. He's gone, and he's not coming back." My lip quivered at her harsh words and I tried to hold back tears.

"Anyway, before I was rudely interrupted, I was trying to tell you about this cute girl I met," Jenna continued and her tone abruptly changed back to one filled with positivity and weightlessness from before I brought up our father.

I tried to listen as she told me about her crush. I

nodded along and gave an enthusiastic "oh wow" and "that's cool" comment when she talked about the things she had to do for the sorority. But I couldn't get back to the optimistic attitude I felt at the beginning of our phone call. Her cold and abrasive response to me mentioning my dad stung deep inside my chest.

As soon as we said goodbye and hung up, I crumbled to the floor in a pile of tears. "I must have forgot," I say to my mom now, who is putting the finishing touches on my hair.

It's perfect—my long waves accented nicely but not too much, so they fall low over my shoulders. It looks natural, only much calmer than the usual frizz and puffiness I have to manage on a daily basis. She pins the top of it back with a shiny, silver butterfly clip. A few strands hang out over my cheeks and makes me look elegant in a way I never have before.

"It looks amazing, Mom, thank you." She sets both of her hands on my shoulders and gives me a light squeeze. I see her gaze in the reflection of the mirror and her eyes are starting to water.

"Are you okay?" I ask her, concern spreading over my features.

"Oh, I'm fine sweetie," she tells me. "You look so beautiful. I hope tonight is everything you want it to be and more."

I smile back at her and watch as she leaves the bathroom, allowing me to do my makeup in peace. What did I want tonight to be? Another loaded question with too many possible answers.

I finish applying a thin coat of eyeliner along my lids when my own reflection catches my eye. Something twists deep in my stomach and I try to push the feeling away. Sparkly silver eyeshadow dances across my lids, my dark brown eyes accentuated at the intensity of the color. The eyeliner lines them and swoops off the side of my eye in a perfect wing, lowering my gaze to my cheeks, where a soft rose-colored blush highlights my bones.

Something's missing.

I cover my lips with a coat of strawberry Chapstick before running over them with a wand of shiny lip gloss. I hate lipstick, and never understood how girls my age got so obsessed with it. It feels like a coat of thick paint on my mouth and prevents me from being able to drink or eat anything whenever I wear it. What's the point? Blotting my lips together on a tissue, I look back into the mirror. *There, that's better.*

But it's not.

No matter how much makeup I put on my face, no matter how long I stare at my reflection, I can't shake the feeling that something is wrong.

The girl in the mirror has the same brown hair as I do, the same brown eyes so deep they could be the color of chocolate, and yet... there's something about her. Something about the way she sits upright bothers me. How the glow of her tan skin looks dimmer, duller than before.

She's staring back at me now, almost desperate, pleading for me to acknowledge her. But I can't.

Because I don't recognize her at all.

Chapter Nine

"Babe, come on! We're going to be late," Jordan screams at me from the bottom of the stairs.

"I'm almost ready!" I yell back at him.

I finally put the finishing touches on my face, going for a classic but elegant makeup look that makes me look sophisticated and older, but not too much older. The silver sparkles of my eyeshadow are still holding strong, but I stuff the small container—along with the eyeliner and my lip gloss—into my black clutch to be safe.

The nerves are practically flowing through every vein in my body as I move to the top of the stairs to make my entrance. My sparkly ombre blue dress fluffs out and hits right above my knees, and the strapless top makes my boobs look much bigger than they really are. Jordan will appreciate that.

If all goes well tonight, I will no longer be a virgin. I'll be Jordan Tucker's girl, in every way that counts. I still don't know if I'm ready but I know I don't want to lose what Jordan and I have. I don't want anything to change.

"Damn," I hear Jordan say as I start my descent down the staircase of my house. He's standing at the bottom next to my mom, who has her phone out and is snapping pictures like there's no tomorrow. He's wearing a white tuxedo, and although we fought a lot about that choice, it doesn't look that bad on him. The light blue bowtie matches the hue of my dress, so it's good enough for me.

The feeling of something missing from earlier returns and I find myself looking around, a pit growing in my heart at not seeing my dad standing here with them.

The only time he got to see me in a dress like this, was for my fifth grade piano recital. It was a pink and fluffy long sleeve thing and made my arms itch like crazy. I hated that dress almost as much as I hated playing the piano, which my mom forced me to do after telling her I didn't want to join choir. My mind takes me back there without any warning.

"You look beautiful, baby!" my dad said to me and squeezed my hand while we sat in the cold, metal chairs in the auditorium of my elementary school. I was next up to play and I wanted to do practically anything else.

"Do I really have to go up there?" I asked my dad.

"You don't want to play?" he asked me and I shook my head. "But you worked so hard on your song."

"I hate playing. I only do it because Mom makes me."

He smiled at me and squeezed my hand again. He briefly looked around the room and then back at me, a grin spreading over his face.

"Well, I don't see Mom anywhere. Do you?"

I smiled a grin so wide it matched the one on his face, and he nodded his head towards the back door. We crept low to the ground to not get in the way of the other attendees and started running to the car once we were outside. I felt like a ninja or a secret spy in a movie.

"I'm feeling a double chocolate chip from Wally's for dinner. What about you?" He rubbed his stomach like he was starving.

"I want one!" I yelled and climbed into the backseat of his car. He told me that in a few years, he would let me ride up front. Right next to him. I couldn't wait to do that.

We drove straight to Wally's Ice Cream Shop and

stuffed our faces with the biggest chocolate chip cookie sandwiches we could find. My dad laughed as I made a mess of chocolate and vanilla ice cream on my face, and I used the bottom of my dress to wipe it away. Mom would definitely notice that.

"Shh," he said to me. "This is our little secret. Okay, princess?"

"Okay, Daddy." I smiled at him and took another bite of ice cream.

"Babe, you look so hot," Jordan says, snapping me back to reality as I reach the bottom of the stairs. I blink a few times to get my bearings and a tear escapes from the corner of my eye as he leans in to kiss my cheek. My face feels flushed and I mentally kick him for doing that in front of my mom. She's never going to let me live this down.

He grabs my arm and wraps a small group of flowers around my wrist. *I've never seen a corsage before*, I think to myself as I notice how the ribbons intertwined in the flowers match the colors of my dress perfectly. Jordan really must have gone out of his way to pick this one out. The intensity of the gesture makes me smile.

Tonight really was going to be everything I dreamed it to be, even without my sister here. Even with the pressure of what I need to do after the dance.

My mom goes into the kitchen and comes back with Jordan's boutonniere, and it takes me almost ten attempts of pinning it onto his jacket before he moves my hands away and does it himself. He seems annoyed by this but then goes right back to smiling for my mom's camera.

"You both look so adorable!" she squeals.

We stand there for a few more minutes taking photos. Some classic poses where Jordan stands behind me and wraps his arms around my waist, and some funny ones where I jump on his back and stick out my tongue.

"We'll take some more at the dance, I promise," I say to my mom.

I hear the honk of a horn and lots of screams from outside the door when my mom finally wraps it up and we say our goodbyes. Outside, the biggest white limo I've ever seen greets us and two of Jordan's friends are sticking their heads out of the moonroof. Both of them are also wearing white tuxedos.

"Ow ow!" they scream as Jordan spins me around on the doorstep for show. I blush almost immediately; I love how he always wants to show me off. He hasn't done it in a while, and the act makes me feel good about myself.

"Damn, Lex, way to make it easy for him!" yells Jake, one of Jordan's teammates.

I don't understand what he means by that, but I slide into the limo with Jordan following behind me. I want to ask him about what Jake said, but he doesn't come sit next to me.

Instead, he plops down in between Jake and Paige, who smiles at me slightly before turning her gaze to Jordan. She looks breathtaking, as always. Her floor-length orange dress hugs her in all the right places and the color glows against her dark skin effortlessly. Her blonde hair is pinned up in a bun that's a combination of both messy and chic. I immediately feel small and dull in comparison to her. The brief moment of confidence from before is gone, replaced with jealousy and bitterness.

Paige always makes me feel inferior. I hate it.

The music in the limo gets louder and I almost don't hear Jordan whisper to Jake from where I'm sitting, but somehow, I do.

"I cannot wait to rip that thing off," he says.

"It's about damn time, dude," Jake replies, and they bump each other's fists.

There are a few other girls in the limo, the other guys' dates, but I don't recognize most of them. Jordan told me that the guys on the team liked to bring girls from other schools, so they didn't mess up their chances for the rest of the year with any of the girls at our school. It doesn't make sense to me, but I'm not one to judge.

Becca is riding to the dance with her friends from the theater club, and Blaze opted out of the whole homecoming thing altogether, which is a surprise to basically no one here.

"Let's get this party started!" Jake screams and pops open a bottle of champagne, most of the white foam spraying on all the girls and their dresses. They don't seem to mind, taking a glass that Jake hands them and sipping away.

As Jake hands me a glass and slings his arm over my shoulder playfully, I look over at Jordan who is too busy talking to Paige to even notice what his friend is doing to his girlfriend. Jake has never talked to me before, let alone touched me. The strong scent of his vanilla cologne is overpowering. My gag reflex kicks in and I do my best to cover it up with a cough.

Something about the way Jordan laughs at what Paige is saying, or how his eyes momentarily glance over her entire body, makes my stomach churn. I grab the glass from Jake and quickly down the golden liquid inside.

The bubbles go straight to my nose, and it feels like I need to sneeze and burp at the same time. Champagne is never at parties—it's always beer. While this tastes much better than beer, I find out the hard way it's not a drink meant to be chugged.

Jake screams in response to my empty glass and

my skin starts to feel warm. I grab the bottle from his hands and take another big gulp directly from the top. For a minute I wonder if the fizz will float to my head and I giggle at the idea of my brain being briefly filled with bubbles.

This gets Jordan's attention, and he leaves Paige's side to come over and sit next to me in the limo. I immediately pull his face to my own and push my tongue against his, claiming him for everyone to see. The entire limo erupts into screams, but Paige looks down at the ground.

He's mine, I mentally tell her. And tonight, I'm going to prove that the only way I know how.

****

We walk into the school's gymnasium and the bright LED lights shining into my eyes from every corner of the room are immediately overwhelming. This year's homecoming theme is "Under the Sea" and it turns out to be as cliche as it sounded. Upon entering, there are colorful balloon arches that have long streamers hanging down, as if they are seaweed we have to push out of our way. Blue and green streamers line the ceiling, and the wooden floor of the gym has a reflection of the ocean, as if we're walking directly into the waves.

A few tables are set up near the back and each one is draped with a light blue tablecloth and a seahorse centerpiece, surrounded by a mix of different seashells. The dance floor is towards the front of the gym by the stage, where a DJ booth sits in a makeshift pirate ship that looks like it's made out of cardboard. To the left of the stage, there's a photobooth area that consists of a blue backdrop and a few girls are already there taking photos, some with fake pearls around their necks and others holding up a realistic looking mermaid tail skirt.

Whatever I thought about homecoming, I have to

admit this is impressive. I can't imagine being on the committee to plan something like this, or how stressful it must be to actually execute the event itself.

"Babe, you match the decorations perfectly." Jordan smiles at me as he leads me to the dance floor.

I glance down at my blue dress and almost regret the color for a minute. Where Paige stands out in her bright orange gown, I blend in instead. For some reason, that makes me sad.

Jordan and I dance together for a while, holding each other to the slow songs and spinning each other around at the fast beats. After a while, I start to get tired and ask him if we can sit down to get something to drink.

"I'll be right back," he says as I get comfortable in a gold Chivari chair at one of the seahorse tables. The back of the chairs are draped in even more streamers, and it makes them look like jellyfish. Even with my love for the beach, this ocean theme is starting to be a little too much.

My feet are hurting so bad, so I kick off my heels and lay my head down on the table before Jordan comes back with our drinks.

"If it's that boring, why did you come in the first place?" a familiar voice asks me.

I look up to see Cameron, standing in front of the table and staring back at me. His normally tousled hair is slicked back in a way that doesn't seem fitting for him, and his black suit is so tight, even I can tell he's uncomfortable. But damn, does he look good.

Nope, you do not think this boy is attractive whatsoever. You despise this boy, remember?

Right.

If my feet didn't hurt so damn bad, I would've gotten up and left at his presence. But I really am not sure if I can shove my toes back into those heels. *I knew I should've worn my Converse.*

"I'm not bored, I'm taking a break. I don't know if you noticed, but I've been dancing with my boyfriend. You know, Jordan Tucker?" I smirk at him.

"Ah, yes, the quarterback. I guess congratulations are in order?"

My heart stops and my face turns pale. How could he possibly know about our plans for tonight? My throat goes dry and I worry for a moment I'm going to be sick. However he found out, I'm sure he thinks the worst of me because of it. But why am I suddenly worried about what he thinks of me? He's nobody to me. My confusion must be clear because he opens his mouth to speak again.

"For winning the game. The other team was our rival right?" he looks at me as though I'm the one not making any sense.

The game, right. I breathe a sigh of relief. "Yes, it was a big win. I'll be sure to tell Jordan you think so."

The mention of the game reminds me of how I completely missed the moment we won, because I was standing at the opposite end zone with Cameron. *Not only standing there*, I remind myself. *You were totally about to kiss him*. I look at him intently, wondering if bringing that moment up causes him to feel anything the way it does for me. By the way he continues to stare at me, I know I'm wrong. Something drops inside my chest at the realization.

I thought he's nobody to you?

I try to hush the voice inside my head and think of something clever to say to get Cameron to walk away. The longer he stands here, the more jumbled my thoughts become.

"Speaking of Mr. Big Time, where is he now? I thought he learned his lesson about leaving his girl alone." And there's the Cameron I despise so much.

Right on time.

I hold back my instinct to grab my heel and throw it at this kid's smug face. But his words make me glance around, and I realize I don't see Jordan anywhere. The drinks table is empty, and he isn't on the dance floor. Where *did* he go?

"Excuse me." I grab my heels in my hand, still not too sure if they would go back on my feet, and push past Cameron. When I do, my shoulder grazes against his and that same electric shock runs down my arm.

I ignore the weird feeling and think he must have been rubbing his feet on a carpeted area or something, as I walk around the stage to find my boyfriend. When I'm on the opposite end of the DJ booth, there are voices coming from the left of the stage. No, not only voices. I hear giggling.

I quickly walk up the stairs and step behind the curtain, out of view to the rest of the homecoming dancers. It's so dark back here, I can barely see in front of me—until I spot the glow of what looks like a phone's flashlight.

But what the flashlight reveals makes me stop dead in my tracks. A bright orange dress cascading off her perfectly symmetrical body and barely touching the floor. Her bare leg wrapped around the back of another pair wearing white pants. The curtains of one of the stage wings covering them enough so they're hidden from the others attending the dance.

Paige.

Paige is kissing Jordan.

"What the hell?" I scream, not sure if it's directed at him, at her, or at both of them.

Jordan pushes Paige off his body so fast, it takes me a moment to register how intertwined they really are with each other. Paige pulls her dress down as if it's an inconvenience, and not like she got caught making out with her friend's boyfriend.

"Lex, I—" Jordan starts to say, but Paige cuts him off.

"I told you if you didn't do something, you were going to lose him to someone who would," she says coldly. That's not exactly what she said, I think to myself. But clearly I've been right all along. She's had an ulterior motive this entire time.

"But you're my fr-friend," I try to say, but the tears are falling from my face faster than I want them to. I know how pathetic it sounds the moment the words leave my mouth. She scoffs a laugh at me and I reflexively take a step back.

"You and I both know we were never friends," she spits at me. I can't argue with that. But this still doesn't make any sense.

"Then why even warn me about Jordan? Why not let him break up with me?" I find my strength to ask her, though there isn't much of it I can muster.

"Jordan was mine, until you came along and thought you could have the world handed to you for being his shiny new toy." Her eyes narrow at me. "I saw right through you—you never loved him. You used him to get popular and get into all of our parties. I had to work hard to be who I am now, but it was all handed over to you and you didn't even want it. None of this meant anything to you. And we gave in because everyone pitied you. 'Oh, poor Lexie, her daddy died. Oh, what a sad situation, her family is barely holding it together' *Bleh!* I was so sick of it." She points a finger to her throat and mimics a gag.

My feet are frozen in place and I can't move. I stare from her to Jordan, who's hiding behind Paige and holding his hands up in the air as if he doesn't want to get in the middle of it.

"Are you seriously not going to say anything?" I ask him.

"I don't know what you want me to say, Lex. I mean, I like you but... Paige is pretty hot." *Is he serious?* I can't believe this is happening.

"But-but we had plans. For after the dance," I can barely get the words out, I can't even say the word I'm looking for.

"Oh, please, like you were actually going to sleep with him," Paige scoffs. "It was never going to happen. Stop pretending and admit it."

Something in between a gasp and a sob breaks out from the back of my throat. A brief moment of reality crashes into me and forces my legs to move out from under me. I don't want to be standing here with either of them anymore. Still clutching my heels, I turn and start to run down the steps of the stage.

"Good riddance," I hear Paige say, but I don't stop running.

I don't stop when Becca yells my name, or when a few of my classmates whisper around me. I keep running towards the door and am only stopped when I collide with what feels like a brick wall. I fall to the floor and my heels slip from my grip. My dress poofs out when I land, my bare thighs burning against the gym floor and a bruise already forming on my tailbone. At least I'm already crying as the pain shoots through my body.

"Whoa, Alex, are you okay? What happened?" I look up and find myself staring into a pair of eyes so reflective of the ocean they could've been a part of the homecoming decor.

"Oh, perfect, just perfect!" I say my thoughts out loud, and grab my heels as I make my way back to my feet. Cameron reaches his hands out to help me up, but I swat them away. I'm so tired of running into him. *Literally*.

"Stop! You can say it already." I stare at him, but he continues to look at me with a blank expression.

"I just caught my boyfriend making out with someone who was supposed to be my friend. So go on, say 'I told you so.' I know you're dying to."

He continues to stare at me and starts to look around us, as if he's trying to see Paige and Jordan for himself.

"Well? Hurry up, already," I urge him on.

"Alex, no. I'm not going to say that because it's not what I'm thinking. Are you okay?" he asks me again.

"Do I look like I'm okay?"

My scream comes out hoarse, and I know I probably look at least half as crazy as I feel. So much for thinking that Jordan would *never* pull a *Carrie* on me.

Cameron reaches a hand out to me, but I shrink back, avoiding his touch. He softens his expression as if the rejection physically causes him pain. Even in my broken state, my heart clenches at his reaction. I'm still so angry with him, but a part of me is also glad he's the one I ran into. I can't imagine it being anyone else. At least I don't care what Cameron thinks of me at this moment.

"Look, I'm sorry that happened and I know this is probably not what you want to hear, but it's for the best. Can you honestly tell me you're this upset about it?"

"Excuse me?" I stare at him incredulously.

Right when I think I'm relieved by his presence, he goes and says something that changes my mind completely. He really is starting to get under my skin and I'm completely over it.

"Come on, I mean—I know you, you don't really care about all this stuff. The quarterback, the popularity.

It's not important." He waves his hand in the air and it reminds me of when we were at the park, talking about this same exact thing but about *him* and not me.

The anger surges through me faster than I can blink and I don't have time to take a breath before I'm reacting.

"Let me remind you," I say as I step closer to him, not giving a crap about how I can feel the heavy lines of mascara and eyeliner flowing down my face. I instinctively rub my hand over my eyes, and the back of it comes away covered in black and silver sparkles. *So much for that long-lasting eyeshadow.*

Cameron's body reflexively leans in closer to me and I watch as he intakes a quick breath. The movement alone makes my head spin and for a moment I forgot what I was about to say. That spark comes to life when I look into his eyes—a hint of tragedy, although now it looks more like desperation. I know if I don't leave now, I'm going to fall apart completely.

"Let me remind you," I say again to emphasize my words without the distraction of what his gaze does to my heart. "You don't know *anything* about me."

I push past him, my shoulder lightly brushing against his own as I storm out of the gym and into the cool night air.

The electricity in my veins and the ache in my gut follows me the entire way home.

ANDIE L. SMITH

Chapter Ten

I'm on my way, the text from Blaze read a little over half an hour ago.

I came straight home from the dance in an Uber, and didn't even bother to wake up my mom. She expects me to be out all night, even though it's only 10:15 right now. Blaze should be here any minute, so I decide to clean myself up the best I can. It takes about six makeup wipes to clear off the mess that is my face, and after a quick use of my Proactiv cleansing brush, I almost feel like a new person. Almost.

The expression on my face causes my stare to linger and for a moment, I start to feel like I know the girl in the reflection of the mirror. But then another tear escapes from the corner of her eye, and the moment passes. I'm not sure if I'm ever going to understand who's looking back at me.

"Okay, what the hell happened?" Blaze marches into my bedroom and at the sight of her, I start sobbing all over again.

Every detail of the night comes rushing out, from the romantic dancing, to the rude interruption from Cam, to the part she wants to hear most about, but I don't think I can say out loud. Somehow, I do.

"Are you kidding me? I'm going to go give that girl a reason to get a new nose job," Blaze says and starts to get up from where we're sitting on my bed.

The response makes me laugh and I take a deep breath, wiping at my face to clear off the rest of the tears that escaped while I was retelling the events of the night to my best friend. It's that moment when I realize the truth to that statement. Blaze is my best friend. Not Paige, or even Becca. Always Blaze. I wrap my arms around her tightly and thank her for being there for me.

"I seriously don't know what I would do without you," I say in her ear.

"Oh, please, you know you would be fine without me. Probably gallivanting the school hallways without a care in the world." She rolls her eyes at me.

"Shut up, you know that's not true. You're literally the only one holding me together."

She smiles at me and I notice her eyes getting watery, but she engulfs me into her arms so quickly I don't have a moment to acknowledge what I see. That's Blaze, never letting her emotions show. She is so much better at it than I am. But even with her badass exterior, only I know how soft she is on the inside.

In third grade, I found her crying at the top of the slide during recess one day. I had never seen her upset before, even that young. I looked at her and asked her where she was hurt, but she shook her head at me. She said she wasn't hurt. My next thought was that someone said something mean to her, so I asked her what happened. She said no one had come up to her. I was so confused as to why she was sobbing, but I knew I needed to be there for her regardless.

She continued to wail hard when I hugged her tightly and I started to get scared. I went to get our teacher, who helped carry Blaze down from the top of the slide. The teacher called her parents and Blaze went home early that day. I was so confused and hoped she was okay. The next day she was back in school, smiling and laughing as if nothing happened. I waited until recess to ask her about why she was so upset the day before.

"Oh, I get sad sometimes," she said to me with a shrug.

"Sad about what?" I asked her.

"Random things. Like any time when I see a dead

butterfly, or when I think about the time I broke my arm, things like that." I still didn't understand.

"So did you see a dead butterfly yesterday?" I asked. She shook her head, and the confusion in my tiny body grew.

"Then why were you crying alone at the top of the slide?" I pressed her.

"Because that's the only time I can—when I'm by myself."

I squeeze her tightly now, remembering one of the only times I ever saw my best friend shed a tear. I forgot about that moment and secretly wonder how many times since then she's been crying when she's alone. Nobody should ever feel like they have to hide that, to only be weak when no one else is looking.

"Okay, well, this is pathetic," Blaze says after returning the hug. "We are not going to sit here and have a pity party while *they* go off and have the night of their lives. Put your shoes back on, we're going out."

"I don't want to go out, Blaze."

"Which is exactly why you need to go out. Dance. Drink. Kiss a random stranger, I don't know!" She throws her hands in the air and I laugh. Her words remind me of a plot to a Hallmark movie. "Come on, it'll be fun and if anything, it'll at least get your mind off things."

Again, someone telling me I need to move on and get over it. Is this seriously how people deal with problems? Only bawling their eyes out when no one else is around and dancing the night away to ignore reality? I want to scream for a thousand years. I don't know if I'm looking for fun, but getting my mind off of tonight's events is extremely intriguing. I am still in my homecoming dress after all.

"Okay, fine. But I am not putting those pieces of crap back on my feet." I nod to the heels sitting in a pile on my bedroom floor from where I threw them down earlier.

Blaze goes into my closet and comes back out with my old, worn down pair of white Converse. I grin a nod of approval at her and slide them on my feet. *Much better.*

I look over at Blaze and take in her outfit for the first time since she got here. She's wearing a pair of dark leather pants and a red lace top that hangs off her shoulders. Her feet are stuffed into her usual black combat boots, and I struggle to hold back a laugh. *My emo goddess.*

An hour later, we pull up to a club with a blaring neon sign above it that reads "MAD HATTER" in a red so deep, it could have been blood. I've never been to an actual club before, only high school house parties and bonfires. I'm not sure what to expect. Summersville isn't really known for its club scene, so we had to drive a little ways out to find this place. Blaze claims it's new and has great reviews on Yelp. I don't know what to think about using Yelp for club reviews, but I'm not really in a place to question it. I don't even know the proper way to find a club, or even what would qualify it to have good reviews in the first place.

For once, I can admit that I want a distraction tonight. The thought brings me back to the dance and hearing what Paige said about me using Jordan to get over my dad's death. At first, I was shocked and hurt that she would think that. But now that I've had more time to think about it, I'm starting to wonder if there's some truth to what she said after all.

Blaze goes through the valet service at the club, which doesn't surprise me. This girl will never leave her white Lexus in a common parking lot. She grabs the card from the valet, and then we step past the line of people and head straight for the door—where we come face to face with a very large and very burly doorman.

For a moment I worry that our little adventure will stop here. There's no way this man is going to let us into the club. Blaze might look like she could pass for twenty-five, but I have a baby face and definitely look like I'm still fifteen years old instead of seventeen. I watch as Blaze leans in like she's going to hug the man, though I notice as she whispers something in his ear and slips a twenty-dollar bill into his front jacket pocket. He smiles at her and holds out his arm, gesturing for both of us to head inside. *Huh, so that really works.*

After we walk in, we both stop immediately.

"Oh, my—" I start to say.

"God!" Blaze finishes, summing up our shock.

"I know, right?" a girl says to us as we walk further into the club. She looks older, probably actually *is* around twenty-five or so, and is dressed in all black from head to toe, sporting some very scandalous fishnet stockings. Her jet black hair is cropped in a pixie cut and she has piercings all over her face. Her nose, her lip, even her eyebrow. *That one probably hurt the worst*, I think.

"Come with me, ladies, I know where to get the best seat in the house."

I don't know if it's my lack of club experience or maybe my lack of legal age, but this is officially the coolest place I've ever been. The building seems so small on the outside, but once you get inside, the space completely transforms.

To the right is an enormously long bar shaped like the trunk of a tree, with ebony-streaked roots growing up from the floor. Behind the bar are a row of black and red mirrors, cut into triangular pieces and intricately pieced together to form some sort of abstract design. When we walk by, I notice how each mirror distorts my face in a different way. It's like being in a funhouse at a carnival, the mirror maze that's always impossible to find a way out of.

As we walk across the dance floor, I look down to see mirrors, again, only this time they change color and light up to the beat of the music coming from the front of the room. These ones aren't protruding distorted images and I'm glad, thinking how that could be problematic for the people dancing above them. I look over to see a small stage at the front of the dance floor and see it's similar to the bar, ebony tree roots mangled across the floor as if they are the only thing holding up the DJ booth. The DJ was pressing buttons on the board in front of him, a dark top hat positioned on his head at an angle.

People all around us are crowding the dance floor, moving to the beats and tossing drinks back into their mouths. Everyone is laughing and having a great time. The atmosphere is electric and intoxicating. I want to be a part of it.

To the left of the dance floor is a row of tables, each one decorated with either red or raven colored roses and Chiavari chairs to match. The center of each table has an object of some sort, each one different from the rest. I squint my eyes as I catch a glimpse of a deck of cards, a caterpillar, and what looks like a very fat cat. The girl—I'm not sure if she's a waitress or a hostess—leads us past the row of tables and towards the back of the room, where two corner booths are arranged to face each other. They are met in the middle by a dark table with, again, tree roots for legs. The seats of the booths are red and more triangular mirrors are surrounding the backing. Luckily, these aren't giving off any weird distortions either. The entire place gives off serious Alice in Wonderland vibes, but much darker and twistier. I feel like a VIP, and for once, I'm okay with it.

"Welcome to the Mad Hatter," the girl says with a chuckle as we stop at the booth. "We hope you are as mad as the rest of us."

My Alice in Wonderland vibes were spot on. And I'm definitely not mad about it.

"What is this place?" I ask, too stunned to even hear the answer.

We sit down in the booth closest to the back wall and I watch as more waiters dressed in all black are walking around, carrying drinks on their trays. Each drink is a different color, and each one has an ice cube inside of it that lights up in a rainbow of colors, changing to a different one every three seconds. I hear the girl—Vera, her name tag reads—explaining something about the meaning of the mirrors to Blaze, but I can't focus on her words too much because I meet the eyes of a guy at the bar. Dressed in the same attire and colors, I almost mistook him for a waiter but with his fedora and—*was that a mask?*—covering his face, I revoke my initial thought.

Nope, no way. I am not here for a guy, that's the exact thing I came here to forget about, so I try to look away from the intensity of his stare.

Vera leaves us at the table, but a few moments later, another waiter comes over and drops off two drinks, each one a different color. I grab the first one he puts down—blue, and sip the whole thing through the straw in a matter of minutes. The overpowering taste of sugar makes me wince as the alcohol flows through my body.

Blaze catches on to my attitude, though for the wrong reasons, and tells the waiter to bring back another round. By the time I've downed almost two blue drinks, I'm starting to feel good. So good, I know that coming here is exactly what I needed to do. I haven't thought about Jordan or Paige once, or anything closely related to what happened tonight. I feel loose, free… for the first time in a long time. I want to make the most of it.

Before I can, though, something makes me pull out my phone and check Jordan's Instagram page, where I see he posted a story over an hour ago. He's at a bar with a group of people. Two girls sit on either side of him in the following selfie, one of them being Paige, and they are both leaning in to kiss his cheek on either side. The way my stomach churns makes me realize I'm not doing a good enough job at what Blaze brought me here to do.

I quickly check Twitter, even though a voice in my head tells me I probably shouldn't. I can't help it, I click over to Jordan's profile. He last tweeted thirty minutes ago, only half an hour after the Instagram story.

This weekend has been full of big wins and beautiful girls.

Gross. I swallow a gulp and suppress the urge to be sick all over the table in front of me. My stomach deserves better than this.

"Is it time to dance?" I hear my voice slur to my best friend and toss my phone back into my bag.

Blaze immediately gets up after taking the last sip of her yellow drink. I grab her hand and head down the walkway from our booth to the main floor of glass lights. The DJ plays some of our favorite songs, and some music with no singing at all. The beat feels amazing through the glass at my feet, and I see why people want to go to clubs all the time.

The vibrations of the music bounce off my skin and sway into the neon lights like I'm in another world. The rush of movement and bodies around me makes me feel so many things at once.

Dizzy. Light. Free.

Drugs aren't my thing, but I could seriously get addicted to this.

Blaze and I dance to so many songs I lose count, and then eventually I lose *her* in the crowd. Somewhere between her hooking her arms around my neck and spinning around to shake her ass at me, a guy from the bar catches her attention and she's out of my sight. The smart thing to do would be to go back to the booth and wait for her, but I don't want to lose the way I feel right now, so I continue to dance by myself. A few guys come up from behind me and try to dance with me… or mostly on me, but luckily, I'm able to shimmy myself away from them.

As soon as I do, I wonder what's wrong with me. I came out here to have a good time, right? So why not have a little meaningless fun, too? Isn't that what Jordan and Paige were doing right now? I mentally tell myself that if another guy comes up to me, I will dance with him and partake in whatever comes after, too. It can't be worse than watching Jordan and Paige suck face behind a stage curtain.

Almost immediately as the thought leaves me, warm, strong hands wrap around my waist. I pause for a moment, doubting if I will go through with this, as the hands spin me around to face my conquest. A small gasp escapes my lips when I look at him. It's the guy from the bar, the one in the mask.

My head tilts in confusion and I think what better way to forget and let go, than with a masked man. He takes my hands and as I wrap them around the back of his neck, his own make their way back to my waist. Hovering over what should be an unsafe area, I feel only certainty and no hesitation in his grip. He probably dances with girls like this all the time. The thought makes me nervous and I'm suddenly hoping my inexperience isn't obvious.

We dance like this for about two songs before a

waiter comes by with a tray holding two glowing shot glasses encompassing some sort of yellow-colored liquid. *Thank God.* I raise my eyebrows at the masked stranger as I down one, holding out the other for him. This time I do sense his hesitation, but he smiles and swallows the liquid in one gulp. For a moment I catch myself seeing Cam in his smile, but the thought quickly disappears as the tequila stings the back of my throat.

The music picks up and with the fresh shot of alcohol burning through my veins, I turn around and start to dance with my partner the way he's probably been expecting me to all along. I look up to see Blaze gaping at me from the bar as I bend over, moving down to the floor and then back up along the man's body. I spin back around to face him only to be met by his lips on mine, and I swear I can hear physical applause coming from the bar.

His kiss catches me off guard, and his mouth is warm and heavy against my own. I break away almost as soon as he does it, and stare at him long enough to see my crazy self reflected in his eyes. This is so not me. *This is something Paige would do.* But isn't that the exact reason why I'm here? Because Paige was off somewhere doing exactly this, with my *boyfriend.* It clearly doesn't matter to them, so why should it matter to me?

Screw it, I think. It's time to give them a little kiss of their own medicine.

With that thought in mind, my next move is a no-brainer. The masked man is staring back at me and looks impatient, and I know if I don't make a move now, he could easily walk away to find someone else to dance with. Not happening, sir. This is my night.

I smile wryly and put my hands back around the base of his neck, pulling his face to mine. My lips crush into his and I'm met with a sweeter kiss than before. He tastes like tequila and a hint of cherry soda. I find myself wanting to taste more of it than I imagined I would have.

His mouth meets the movements of my own with a new sense of urgency, as if he's expecting the kiss to end at any moment. His muscular arms wrap completely around my waist and as they press my body into his own, it's as if we have become one person instead of two. Everywhere he touches leaves a line of electricity on my skin and shocks are running all the way down to my toes. As his hands find my hair and eventually grab the sides of my face, I'm all too aware of how amazing this feels.

I lose myself in the music and rhythm of our lips intertwining, so I almost don't hear it when the masked man whispers my name. If I had slurped down one more glowing drink, maybe I wouldn't have even heard it at all. But I do, and I immediately break away from his grasp.

"I-I never told you my name." I panic and back up.

When his hand reaches for my own, I immediately recognize the familiarity of his strong grip and how his touch sends sparks along my arm.

No. *It can't be.*

But when I look up to notice the eyes of my perfect stranger, I realize that it is.

The color of the ocean marked with a pain so deep, you had to look away. I know those eyes.

Cameron.

ANDIE L. SMITH

Chapter Eleven

Cameron runs out of the club so fast that at first, I don't even notice that he walked off the dance floor. I'm still trying to catch my breath and wrap my head around what the hell just happened. After I pushed away from him, I ran back up the stairs to where Blaze is now sitting in our booth. When I turn around to glance back at him, he's gone.

"Alex, are you okay?" Blaze asks as I sit down at the corner booth. "Who was that?" I am not okay, but I have no idea how to tell her that or how to explain what had happened. For all she knows, I did exactly what she said I should do to get my mind off of Jordan. I went out. I danced. I kissed a random stranger. Check, check, check.

Only he wasn't random. And he certainly wasn't a stranger. But Blaze doesn't know this.

"No one, that was definitely no one and I have no idea what that was, so we are not talking about this ever again," I say to her quickly.

Blaze catches on to my hysteria and nods like she knows exactly who it was, but gives my hand a squeeze to tell me she won't press the issue any further. There's no way she could know, but I appreciate the sentiment. I take a deep breath and throw my head back against the rim of the booth.

"This was fun and all, but I think I'm about done. Can we go?" I ask.

She nods her head and we gather our things to walk out the door of the club. I half expect Cameron to be standing out here, waiting for me to chase after him, but when I walk outside, I'm met only by the chill air of the night and a super smiley valet attendant. We hand Mr.

Smiley the ticket and his tip then wait as he brings Blaze's Lexus up front to us. I get in the passenger side, thanking Blaze for not drinking nearly as much as I did and being able to drive us home.

"Do you want to talk about it?" she asks me, turning down the radio as we pull out of the club's parking lot.

"Not really, no. I want to go home and take a shower before I crash," I reply.

She nods and turns the music back up a few notches and I roll down the window to get some fresh air on my face. The last ten minutes of the night replay in my head and either way I think about it, my brain can't seem to come around to what happened.

"I don't understand how he was here! How could he have known where I was, or even find the club in the first place," I say out loud. "Why won't he leave me alone? And what was with that mask? What are we, playing some game of *Cinderella*?" I instantly laugh at my comment, thinking of how stupid I am.

Growing up, *A Cinderella Story* was my favorite movie. Not all the remakes about dancing or singing, but the original movie with Hilary Duff and Chad Michael Murray. I always made fun of her Prince Charming and how he had zero clue who she was because her face was covered by a tiny little mask. I never understood how he didn't notice her eyes, hair, or even height to realize who she was. Well, I guess now I know how Charming feels. *I am such an idiot.*

Blaze doesn't respond, she knows better than to indulge me and my quips. I roll the window back up and lean my head against it, pretending to sleep for the rest of the ride home while my mind continues to race. After a while, I hear the car's brakes shriek as it comes to a stop and feel Blaze gently shaking my shoulder to wake me up. I blink a few times to mimic the act of waking up and even throw in a little stretch of my arms for some extra convincing.

I lean over the console and hug Blaze goodnight, promising to see her at school on Monday after she asks me three times if I'll be there. I head inside my house and jump straight into bed, not even bothering to change out of my dress despite how uncomfortable it was. The clock on my bedside table reads 4:10 AM, and I'm desperate to sleep the rest of the weekend away before going back to school. *Ugh.* Monday will be here before I know it and I'm dreading it. The entire school will know that Jordan dumped me for Paige. My whole world is about to change, and not in a good way.

And what am I going to do about Cameron? I don't have any classes with him, but that doesn't mean I won't see him at some point. The thought makes me nervous and I reflexively bring my fingers to my lips, which I swear are still tingling from Cameron's kiss. He's the most annoying person I've ever met, but I'd be lying if I said it was a bad kiss. I fold myself under the covers of my bed and drift off to sleep, a deep sea of blues and emerald greens taking over my dreams.

****

"Do you even understand how beautiful you are?" Cameron whispers in my ear.

We're lying on the open field of the recreation center. He's on the ground and I'm resting the back of my head on his chest. We're looking up at the night sky, his fingers absentmindedly playing with my hair. The feeling is so soothing, I know sleep is only minutes away if he keeps going. I smile at him, though he can't see it from how I'm positioned.

"I don't know how I got so lucky."

I prop myself up and turn over on my elbows,

staring into his hauntingly gorgeous face. His emerald eyes gaze back at me and for a moment I lose my breath.

"Stop being cheesy," I laugh at him.

He sits up a little bit so that his face is closer to my own. My heart starts to beat a thousand times over. I love how nervous he makes me feel.

"I can't help it. You make me cheesy."

He lunges forward and tackles me, rolling me over onto the grass and tickling my sides.

"Cameron!" I screech in between a fit of laughter.

We're wrestling for a few minutes before we both stop, clearly out of breath. He's holding himself up, hovering over me. His body is so close to mine I can see his breath catch in his throat, his Adam's apple bobbing up and down once. He's staring at me so intensely, all sense of reality escapes my mind.

"Are you going to kiss me?" I ask him. I need him to kiss me so badly. My body is burning with desire and aching for his touch at the same time.

"Well, it's not as fun if you have to ask for it." He smirks at me.

I playfully shove at his chest, which almost knocks him over from his hold above my body. He laughs and I watch the blues of his eyes twinkle with the sound. My heart flutters as he brings his face closer to the ground, closer to me. His lips are inches away from my own, my whole body frozen in place. I bite my lip in frustration, he's taking too long. I feel him sigh against my mouth and almost come undone from the sound alone.

"Your dad is going to kill me if I don't get you home," he says and leans his forehead against mine.

I sit upright so fast, I knock my head into his with a force harder than I intend to.

"Ouch!" he screams.

"What did you say?" I ask him. Surely, I misheard him.

"I don't want to get on bad terms with your dad. I thought that would make me a good boyfriend, jeez."

I think he's kidding, but the look on his face shows he's dead serious. But that isn't right, my dad is dead.

I glance around at our setting and now see how distorted it really is. The wooden park structure was standing strong to my right side. The castle turrets climbed towards the night sky, and the lanky bridges still connected the two ends of the palace.

But that isn't right, the castle was torn down years ago.

"Alex? What's wrong, babe?" Cameron asks me. I look back at him now and feel nothing but pure confusion wash over me. Babe? He never calls me babe. He barely even knows me, yet now he's my boyfriend?

"Wait. When did we start dating?" I ask him. His response is a surge of laughter as he rises to his feet.

"Come on, you weirdo. Let's get you home."

I grab his hand, standing up and following him back to the parking lot. An actual parking lot, with concrete poured and white lines dividing the parking spaces. Cameron walks over to a car, but I stop short of getting in. It looks brand new, the metallic coat of silver paint shining brightly off the Mercedes logo.

"I thought you drove a Civic," I say to him. Cameron laughs loudly again, and rolls his eyes at me.

"A Civic? Come on Alex, you know me better than that."

No, I don't. He's wrong.
I don't know him at all.
This is all wrong.

ANDIE L. SMITH

Chapter Twelve

Monday morning comes around much faster than I want it to. I slept almost the entire day yesterday, thankfully without any more weird dreams, and I still feel hungover getting out of bed today.

My phone *pings* three times before I finally walk over to check it on my nightstand. Three missed calls from Blaze, wonderful. She probably thinks I'm still asleep and wants to make sure I don't skip today. I've only got about 20 minutes to shower and get dressed before she gets here, so I text her a quick, **getting ready, see u soon**, before starting my daily routine.

By the time I shower and find an outfit that is somewhat acceptable to be seen in public, I try to recall all the events from the weekend and what could possibly happen at school today. My head is throbbing from all the thoughts and confusion roaming around and I realize how desperate I am for a large cup of coffee. I hope I have enough time to make one before Blaze gets here.

Ping. That would be a no.

I'm here, and I already went on Starbucks run so get your butt in the car and let's go the text from Blaze reads.

I gather my things and grab my bag, heading downstairs and locking the door as I leave the house. I have no idea how I'm going to get through school today. Thank God, Blaze already went for coffee. I climb into the passenger side of Blaze's car, murmuring a quick good morning to her. She smiles back at me while handing me my coffee and I'm filled with the delicious scent of white chocolate mocha. If only this smell could simultaneously take away my headache and the agony of the day at the same time.

"No matter what happens, you got me. You know that, right?" Blaze says as we pull up to school. Fortunately, that's the one thing I *do* know about today—and every day, really. I will always have Blaze.

I finish my coffee and I'm grateful for the fresh air as we step out of the car. The silence of the ride was so awkward, and I know Blaze is trying to give me space to prepare for the day ahead. If only it could be that easy.

We walk through the courtyard and Blaze stops next to me, looking over at our group's usual hangout spot in the center of the quad. The entire group is there and in the center of everyone is Paige—sitting on Jordan's lap. She's laughing about something he said and he's twirling a strand of her long blonde hair in his fingers. Suddenly, I feel like my white chocolate mocha is about to make a reappearance. My hands form into a fist, my fingernails pressing hard against the palms of my skin.

Becca notices us and tries to wave us over, but Paige slaps her hand away and stares me down, shaking her head ever so slightly. Her gaze almost says, "don't you dare" and something about it makes me want to strut on over there and tell her exactly what I think about the situation.

But the bell rings, and the moment passes. Paige and Jordan get up from the bench they're sitting on and walk hand-in-hand towards the opposite end of the school. Jordan doesn't even see me.

Blaze physically has to pull my arm to get me moving and I know if I don't, we're going to be late for first-period biology. Not that I really care. Whoever decided that the buttcrack of dawn is the most perfect time to dissect frogs is forever on my shit list.

She squeezes my arm sympathetically and walks past me into the classroom. I sit down at my usual stool next to her, mentally thanking Mr. Salts again for letting us choose our lab partners this year. Our teacher walks in and begins writing something on the board while talking about our lesson for the day. Something about mitosis, I think. Whatever that is. I'm too distracted by Blaze scribbling something on a piece of scrap paper to listen further.

Are you okay? is all the paper says after I unfold it from her sliding it across the table to me. I shrug at her in response and don't bother sending a note back over. Am I okay? I really don't know.

Seeing Jordan and Paige together should have bothered me, it should've made me sad or even angry. But it wasn't seeing them together that pissed me off, it was the smirk on Paige's face that did. And that's only because she thinks she's right about me, and I don't like that.

If they want to be together, let them I scribble down on the paper and pass the note over to Blaze. She glances at me for a moment too long before sending her response back my way.

It's that guy, isn't it? it reads.

Reflexively, I look around the room thinking she means he's here, in our class. My stomach relaxes when I don't see him.

"What are you talking about?" I mouth to her.

She grabs the paper back and starts writing on the other side for what feels like hours, before sliding it back over to me again. I check the clock at the front of the room reading 8:15 AM, and roll my eyes at how slow she writes.

The fact that you don't care about Jordan and Paige. It's because you like this new guy.

I stare at her note for longer than normal, mainly because I don't want to look up and see Blaze's face. She knows me better than anyone and I know the moment I look at her, I will give everything away. And I don't want to admit it.

My eyes are drawn back to the board and I try to listen to Mr. Salts's lecture to avoid thinking about it, but he's talking about different phases of cells and how there are multiple steps in each phase before they can get to the other phase... My brain is hurting and he isn't making any sense.

I sneak a glance at Blaze and unsurprisingly, she's starting right at me. I don't want to admit that I'm crushing on Cameron. Because that would mean I don't love Jordan, that I possibly never truly did in the first place. Which would mean I almost gave up my virginity the other night for no reason at all.

And I do love Jordan. At least, I think at one point I did, but there was always something missing between us that I couldn't quite figure out. Coming to terms with that has me wondering if Paige has been right all along, if my relationship with Jordan never mattered to me.

I know the parties, the sudden popularity, all of that helped distract me from thinking about my dad. But I never considered Jordan to be one of those things. Jordan was a surprise. He just kind of happened, and I went along with it. *Was* he another distraction for me? Did our relationship really not mean anything? I shake my head at the thought. If that's true, that makes me a horrible person. And Paige would be right. I don't want that, she doesn't deserve that satisfaction.

Even so, I can't deny that I'm interested in Cameron, no matter how much I want to ignore it. I don't know if I can say I like him, I mean, the guy drives me absolutely insane and the only times I've been around him I've wanted to punch him in the face, but kissing him the other night changed everything for me.

Even *thinking* about kissing him makes me feel all sorts of things at once, feelings I never had when I was with Jordan. For crying out loud, I'm even *dreaming* about the guy. There's something about him. Like he and I are connected in a way that I can't exactly explain. But I want to be able to explain it, and I can't. It's driving me crazy.

The universe must be playing tricks on me because as soon as I think his name, my phone vibrates in my bag. I quietly place my backpack on my lap and stick my hand in to check the screen, peeking up to make sure Mr. Salts doesn't see me. He'd take away my phone for the rest of the school day if he caught me texting.

When a girl across the room asks a question that prompts our teacher to turn back to the whiteboard, I seize my opportunity to check the message.

Can we talk?—C

It's from Cameron. *Of course it is*. How did he get my number?

I had planned on ignoring him if I saw him in the hallway at school, but here he is making himself known through my phone. Blaze's last note still sits on my binder, the words almost bouncing off the paper like they're mocking me.

I don't know if this is the right thing to do, but I know I want answers. I need to know how Cameron found me at the club the other night, and more importantly, why he kissed me. But mostly, I'm curious if the kiss meant anything to him the way it does for me. And if there's any possible reason for this unexplainable connection I feel to him. There's only one way to find out, so I quickly type my reply and hit SEND before Mr. Salts turns back around to face the class.

Lake Monroe, 4 pm I send him. I place my bag back onto the table and take out a notebook, pretending to listen and take notes of whatever Mr. Salts is saying about cells merging together and then splitting up only to merge again. Again, I wonder if I'm the only one confused here or if he isn't making sense to everyone else in the class.

I glance over at the clock once more, now reading 8:30. *Damn*, it's going to be a long day.

****

I'm sitting in Blaze's Lexus, grateful she let me borrow it to meet Cam this afternoon while she's at her club meeting. I really need to get my own car.

It's starting to get chilly out, so I pump up the heat in the car's air conditioning. Being this late into the year, it's abnormal for it to still be hot out. However, I definitely am not dressed for this sudden drop in temperature today. My ripped skinny jeans provide some warmth, but my burgundy strappy tank top leaves most of my upper body susceptible to the cool air.

I try to calm the nerves in my stomach while I wait for Cameron to show up. Why am I nervous? I barely even know the guy. But no matter how hard I try, I can't shake him. He's everywhere and it's only getting more difficult for me to ignore.

I try to recall my conversation at lunch with Blaze to distract myself until he gets here.

"Cameron? You mean to tell me the guy you have been crushing on this entire time was the one who you were kissing in the club after homecoming and you're only telling me this now?" Blaze stared at me with her mouth open after the accusation.

I didn't want to tell her because I knew this would be her reaction. But between my weird dream about dating him—in which my dad was alive—and then her note in Biology class, I couldn't take it. She was my best friend, and she could tell something was bothering me.

"I'm sorry!" I said to her. "I didn't want to say anything because I didn't even know how I felt about it."

"And how do you feel about it?" she asked me.

"I don't know," I shrugged. "I mean, homecoming was only *two* nights ago. I shouldn't be thinking about Cameron, I should be bawling my eyes out into tubs of ice cream over my boyfriend cheating on me."

"Sure, you *should* be doing all that," Blaze waved a hand in the air. "But you're not. And I think that tells you more than you need to know."

She was right, yet again. All weekend I had tried to be upset about the whole Jordan fiasco. But I wasn't. It sucked, and I was pissed off, but more at Paige than anything. I hadn't really thought about Jordan once. Not since my lips were on Cameron's.

"It was a pretty good kiss." I smiled at Blaze and reflexively brought my fingers to my mouth.

"See! I knew it! You *like* him." Blaze nudged my arm and winked at me.

"Okay, fine! I like him. There. Are you happy?"

Blaze was smiling back at me so big, it was infectious and I had to return the grin. My chest felt a little lighter at the omission, but it didn't take away the confusion I felt at the same time. Sure, I was crushing on Cameron. But would that be enough? He still drove me crazy and I really didn't know that much about him.

The sound of a car engine distracts my thoughts.

My brain must have conjured him up because a moment later, Cameron is pulling into the space next to me in the open field. There isn't really a parking lot at the lake anymore, only a big grassy field to park wherever you want. Since no one really comes here anymore, parking isn't really a big deal.

Cameron gets out of the car, but he doesn't smile, doesn't wave at me. He stares right through the front window as if he's looking out to the other side, straight past me. My body chills at the gaze.

I watch as he walks down to the bank of the lake and I almost wonder if he wants to be alone, if he doesn't even want to talk to me at all. But that's dumb because he's the one who texted me.

When I see his silhouette move to look back towards the car, to me, I know I'm wrong. I get out of the car and walk past him, down the grassy hill to what remains of the old dock, which is still in pretty decent shape despite everything, and sit down at the edge, dangling my feet over and draping my arms through the railing. He follows me a minute after I sit down.

"So—" I start to say.

"Listen—" he says at the same time.

We both laugh at ourselves and the awkwardness in the air lifts. Suddenly, I have no idea what I want to say or how to even start this conversation, so I nod my head at him to go first.

"Let's go ahead and clear the air here, toss the elephant into the water or whatever," he starts.

"What?" His phrase catches me off guard and I can't help but laugh. "You mean the elephant in the room?"

"Well, we aren't in a room. We're on the water. So we are tossing the elephant in the water." One side of his mouth turns up at the corner and it's a good thing I'm sitting down, because that side smile alone could make my knees go weak. He's still standing above me, staring out into the open water ahead of us.

"Blaze gave me your number, for one. She also texted me to come to the club the other night, for two."

I have absolutely no response to that and my brain spins. Blaze talked to him?

I think back on my conversation with her at lunch,

where she acted so shocked when I told her Cameron was the one I kissed in the club. But that wasn't news to her at all. She knew it was him because she's the one who invited him. *Why didn't she tell me?*

"Before you get mad at her, don't. I've known Blaze almost as long as you have. Her parents are tight with my dad, and I've been to more Montgomery birthday parties than you can imagine," he laughs and I join him, thinking about all the crazy parties Blaze's family has thrown for her over the years.

It doesn't slip my mind that I probably have been in the same room as Cameron on more than one occasion. It's too bad I haven't noticed him before. *Wait, did I mean that?*

"Okay, fine. So did Blaze tell you to kiss me, too?" I raise an eyebrow at him.

My question catches him off guard and I watch as he goes to open his mouth, then close it about three different times. Being stumped is a good look on him. Being *anything* is a good look on him. I tighten my grip on the railing in front of me, suddenly worrying about his answer. Did he only kiss me because Blaze told him to? Did it mean anything to him? I don't know why, but I need to know if he felt something from it the way I did.

Crap, I think. I *do* like him.

"No," he says finally. "Blaze did not tell me to do that. That was me, and I got caught up in the moment. Sorry about that."

My heart sinks in my chest. The immediate rejection is like having a pile of cold water splashed against my face. I hate how much it hurts.

"Ah," is all I can think to say. "So then why are you so interested in my popularity?" I ask, trying to change the subject so he doesn't notice the utter disappointment on my face.

Cameron must have been really thinking about how to answer my question because he stays silent longer than I anticipate. What is he hiding? Suddenly, I want to know everything about him. I want him to know me. And that thought scares the hell out of me.

My thoughts are interrupted by his next movement when he finally comes to sit down next to me at the edge of the dock. He hangs his legs over the side to mimic the position of my own, and the close proximity of his skin to mine sends my stomach into a pit of somersaults.

"When I was ten, my mom died."

Now it's my turn to open and close my mouth three times, absolutely speechless. I know better than anyone there is nothing someone can say to make that sentence better. And yet I find myself wanting to do exactly that. The look on his face, so solemn and calm, yet so sad, is heartbreaking.

I'm surprised at how much I miss his smile at that moment, and how I want to do anything to make it return to his face so badly. Being sad is *not* a good look on him. Seeing him sad stirs something inside me I didn't know was there anymore.

"Oh." My voice squeaks and I clear my throat, embarrassed.

He laughs and out of the corner of my eye I see his face turn to look at me. If I look at him at the right angle, our lips would be so close to touching. My heart is beating as if it's going to ricochet right out of my chest. I've never felt so nervous in all of my life. I can't make myself turn my head, though. Something forces me to not take my eyes off the water's edge.

You are not seriously thinking about kissing him right now. God, what's wrong with me?

He's smiling at me. "Thank you."

"For what?" I ask in confusion.

"For not saying the words I don't want to hear. 'I'm sorry for your loss' and all that other bullshit. I'm sure you can understand how annoying all of that is. You more than anyone."

He's right. The only thing that sucks more than losing someone you loved is everyone else around you acting like they know what you're going through. They don't, but it makes them feel better to pretend like they do.

"I hate that one the most—when people say they're sorry for my loss. Like I misplaced my dad in the same way I could lose my headphones or something. I know what they mean, but it still bothers me," I say to Cameron.

My body goes rigid as the words leave my mouth. I've never said that before, to anyone. Saying it out loud is like a breath of fresh air.

For a moment, I worry that Cameron is going to laugh at me, make fun of me for feeling that way. I shouldn't have said it, but I can't help it, I'm so comfortable around him. *Damn this boy and whatever he's doing to my insides.*

"Right?" He nods his head and I instantly feel better. "My favorite is when people ask me if there's anything they can do for me. Because they don't want the real answer. They only want to feel better about themselves. They want me to say 'Oh, no, but thank you so much for asking, it means the world to me!' when in reality, I want to say 'Oh, yeah! You know what would be great, is if you could bring my mom back from the dead. That would be super cool and extremely helpful' but I can't say that. Though it would be pretty funny if I did, maybe once. Whoever I said that to would probably shit bricks."

I try not to laugh, but I can't help it. He's right again. The actual losing someone part is heart wrenching, but the sympathy responses are the worst. No one really wants to know how we're doing. No one wants to hear the truth. They want to feel like they did their part so they can move on with their own lives.

"How did she die?" I ask, focusing the conversation back to his mom.

"She was sick, breast cancer. At the time, I had no idea what that meant. I only knew that I was never going to see her again. Now that I'm older, I've done my research and really understand what she was going through. I wish I could've been there for her."

I shudder at the thought. I can't even imagine watching a parent go through something like that, especially at that age.

"My dad did a great job at hiding a lot of the bad parts. I never saw her throwing up, or even without any hair. Every time we saw her in the hospital, she didn't seem any different to me. She was still my mom." He chokes up a little at the last part.

His vulnerability shakes me at my core and this time I do turn my head. I look over at him and fight the urge to wrap my arms around him, but I am so tempted to close the distance between us.

I can hear the rise and fall of his chest as he breathes. His mouth is only mere inches away from my own, his breath warm against my skin. My forehead creases with confusion as I watch his eyes stare back into mine, and then look down at my lips for a brief moment, so fast I would've missed it if I blinked.

My breathing stops. He really needs to stop doing that.

He surprises me by taking my hand and I immediately jump at the personal contact. I look down at our entwined fingers then back up at his emerald flaked eyes. The intimacy of his touch catches me off guard. He seems so familiar and so strange at the same time. It's like he knows everything about me, only he knows nothing at all. How could I want to spend so much time with someone who drove me halfway insane?

"Life pretty much sucked after she died. Not because she was gone, but because I was so young. A ten-year-old is in no way capable of understanding death the way a seventeen-year-old is." He glances over to me, still holding my hand. "You're lucky in a way."

Suddenly the heat from his touch is so alarming it's like a third-degree burn and not a rush of desire.

"Lucky?" I almost scream at him. Surely he did not say that. But he did.

I quickly let go of his hand and climb to my feet. Any warm and fuzzy feelings I had for him a moment ago are gone, now replaced with anger and bitterness. I cannot believe he said that. He stands up almost as fast as I do, confusion spreading across his face.

"Alex, I—" he starts to say.

"Please, tell me more about how lucky I am that my dad died."

"No, that's not what I—" he starts before I cut him off again.

"Who do you think you are? Following me around, acting like you know me. Well, again, I don't know how many times I have to say it, you don't know *anything* about me," I spit at him. "God, I am so *sick* and *tired* of this. Everyone else acts like my dad didn't even exist in the first place, that his death is no big deal, and now here you are telling me I'm *lucky* he died?"

"Alex, stop!" he yells over me.

The rise in his voice makes me do that and I stare at him expectantly. There isn't much he can say at this point to recover with me. Here he goes again, getting under my skin and reminding me why I shouldn't be interested in him.

"That's not what I meant. When I lost my mom, I was ten years old. Ten!" His voice cracks and even though I don't want it to, my heart almost breaks at the sound.

"I didn't know anything. I didn't know what death meant. I went to the funeral, I visited her grave. But I kept waiting around the front door like an idiot, thinking she would walk through at any moment. Maybe lucky was a bad choice of words," he says and I scoff.

"But what I'm trying to say is... does it suck that your dad died? Yes. Is it probably killing you inside? That's highly likely. But at least you're old enough to know what it means. To process your grief and learn how to live with it. You're old enough to have memories of him, to carry those with you for the rest of your life. I would kill for one single memory about my mom that didn't involve her lying in a hospital bed."

His words send another surge of anger, but also anxiety, and sadness, through my veins. It's something he says that bothers me, but I can't pinpoint what it is. I'm still so mad at him for calling me 'lucky' to think about anything else coming out of his mouth.

"It's not going to work you know." He stares at me openly. "Dating the quarterback, hanging out with those snotty friends of yours. It's not going to magically make your dad come back. He's gone, Alex. And you need to process that. If you don't, you'll only make it worse."

This is too much. All of this is suddenly way too much.

"I don't want to be here anymore." I shake my head and start to walk past him. "And I definitely don't need you telling me what I need to do. Do not even think about following me."

"Alex, please—" He grabs my arm and I flinch at the electricity in his touch. I pull away from his grip abruptly.

"Stop it! For once, please, do what I ask and leave me alone!" The tears are building up faster now and I don't know why, but I don't want him to see me cry. I break into a sprint and climb back into Blaze's car before he can chase after me.

I back out of the field and head onto the main road, back to school to pick up Blaze from her environmental studies meeting. Frantically wiping at my face, it takes everything in me to force the tears back down. For so long, I've been doing what everyone else has told me to do. I've distracted myself, I've ignored any sad feelings—I've done all I can to get over it. To move past it, as my mom told me to do. So why does my body keep fighting me on that? Why can I seem to do anything but?

I park at the school and wait for Blaze to be done with her meeting. My hands dig through the center console and strike gold, pulling out a napkin to blow my nose. Ugh, gross. I take a few deep breaths and try not to think about my interaction with Cameron on the dock. Try to ignore the feeling of his hand in mind. How desperately I wanted to be wrapped in his arms. The way one touch sent my body into a full on electric charge.

I have no idea who I am right now, or what I was thinking by meeting up with Cameron. *I cannot believe I wanted to kiss him again!* My groan is perfectly timed with the moment I throw my head back against the seat. My eyes flutter open, and I see Blaze heading toward the car.

The quick motion of her stride causes her to trip

over a crack in the sidewalk, and she catches herself, but not before her backpack falls off of her shoulders. She bends down to pick up the loose items that fall out of it and the action reminds me of when my sister practically ran off after the night we found out Dad was dead. I close my eyes, overwhelmed at the memory, not sure how much more my emotions can take.

"Where are you going?" I asked Jenna.

I was sitting in my bed, the comfort of my rose sheets and blue duvet wrapped around me like I was a burrito. I didn't want to leave this spot, to go back downstairs and hear my mom crying.

Jenna was rummaging around the room, placing things in her backpack. I watched as she stuffed her toiletry bag, phone charger, and a pair of clothes into her bag. Almost an hour ago, she was taking all that stuff out.

"I need to get back to campus."

"What? I thought you were staying here. At least for tonight," I pleaded to her.

Having Jenna in my room was the only real thing I could focus on. I had no idea what was going on and I didn't know what to believe. I needed Jenna to help me make sense of all of it. Like she always has.

A part of me kept waiting for my dad to walk in the door, laughing and telling us all this was one big joke. But another part of me knew that wasn't going to happen, that this was real. He was really gone.

I didn't want to see my mom's tears and I definitely didn't want to sit with her while she stared at me with those big, sympathetic eyes. I wanted my sister, and she was leaving.

"Jenna, please. We need to be together right now."

She stared back at me with a gaze so intense I shrunk back into my cocoon of blankets.

"We don't need to be anything. I need to get back to campus," she said harshly.

"But Jenna, why? Don't you understand what's going on?" She didn't answer me and a deep feeling of desperation formed in my gut.

"Dad is dead! He's dead, Jenna!" I yelled at her, but was weeping so hard, the words slurred together.

"I know. And I'm sorry for that, I am. But I-I have to go."

She walked out the door so quickly, so focused. It was like she never even wanted to be there in the first place. I couldn't believe her. I was given the worst news of my life. We were given the worst news of our lives. And she acted as if it didn't bother her one bit. She didn't care that our dad was dead. Did he really mean that little to her?

My mom came into my bedroom "Alex? Is everything okay? Jenna said she was leaving.".

"She doesn't care about Dad."

"Now, that's not true." My mom came over and sat on the edge of the bed. Her eyes were rimmed in red, but her face was dry. I thought she would still be upset. "She probably had to get back to school. Maybe she has a big project due or something."

"What project could possibly be more important than finding out your dad died?" I stared at her in disbelief.

She didn't answer me and I realized I didn't even want her to. I couldn't handle the way she was looking at me, like I was some broken toy she was trying to figure out how she could fix.

"When do you think she will come back?" I asked.

My mom froze in place on the bed and her face immediately lost all color. I tried not to laugh when I realized she looked as pale and white as Edward Cullen in the first Twilight movie.

I started to worry. "What is it?"

"I don't think she's coming back, sweetie." What?

"What do you mean she's not coming back? Don't we have to have a funeral or something?"

"Of course we do, but Jenna doesn't have to come if she doesn't want to."

"But it's Dad. Why wouldn't Jenna be there?"

"I think she needs some time to process all of this. She loved your father dearly, as we all did. And now she doesn't know what to do. She needs some space." My mom reached over and put her hand on my shoulder. I was still encompassed in my comforter, so I didn't even feel it when she gave my shoulder a light squeeze.

I didn't understand why Jenna would leave so abruptly. Why wouldn't she want to come back for the funeral?

"So what are we supposed to do now?"

"Oh, sweetie, we will figure it out. We have each other and we have our home." She gestured around the room. It didn't feel like our home anymore, not without my dad in it. "All right, well, I'll leave you be for a while. Maybe we can get breakfast in the morning? Go to that diner you like so much?"

I opened my mouth to say something, but thought better of it, and nodded my head to her. All the energy I had left in me, though it was very little, was completely drained. I felt empty inside and couldn't find anything to say that would come close to making her happy.

She walked out of the room smiling, as if nothing about the last two hours even happened. Was I the crazy one? Was I the one acting out here?

Dad was dead and Jenna left us. Why did it feel

like I was the only one hurt and confused?

"Ah!" I let out a scream of frustration and threw the pillow that was behind my head over the far side of the wall.

It hit my dresser and sent an item sitting on top of it crashing to the ground. I heard the sound of breaking glass and immediately jumped to my feet. No, no, no.

But it was too late. I had knocked over the picture frame holding the photo of my dad and me at a Rascal Flatts concert. I was fourteen in the photo, it was my first concert. One of my favorite memories. He framed it for me as a Christmas present that year, a frame with microphones and speakers on it—fitting given the photo.

My body fell back to the floor and tears fell down my face as I stared at the collection of glass in front of me. I held on to the picture tightly, thankful it didn't rip or tear during the crash. Little pieces of a microphone were scattered all around the floor with other particles of glass. I tried to carefully pick up the pieces without cutting myself, but it was no use.

The frame was broken. And it was never going to look the same again.

The sound of a car door slamming snaps me back to the present and I smile at Blaze when she gets in.

"Everything okay?" she asks me, concern forming over her brow.

I think over her question for a moment before I answer. Everything is most definitely not okay. From my screaming match with Cameron, to Paige and Jordan hooking up, to the way everyone continues to move on with their lives after my dad's death.

And it isn't lost on me that Blaze, my best friend in the entire world, has been lying to me.

I'm going insane, yet no one seems to care.

"Yep. Everything's fine," I say to her.

Because God forbid I'm allowed to say anything else.

Chapter Thirteen

"I don't know about this, Blaze," I say to her as she walks around my room, rummaging through my drawers while I sit on the edge of my bed. She throws a pile of jeans over to me, but it's a pair that isn't my size anymore, so I get up to go put them back in my drawer.

"Oh, come on, you don't have to break up with the parties because you and Jordan called it quits. Besides, it's Bev's party." She has a point there.

Bevlyn Richards is the most popular senior at our school and every year, she throws a party when her parents go out of town for the weekend, sometimes multiple times a year. Everyone who is anyone at school knows about her parties and even those who don't somehow end up crashing anyway. Her parties are not ones you want to miss, and the last time I went to one was at the beginning of the school year, right after I started dating Jordan.

Bev and I were never really friends, but we ran in the same circles of popularity, so we socialized a lot. At the first party I went to with Jordan, we got there early and I actually offered to help her set up before the other guests arrived. She laughed at me and told me she "had people for that" but said it was cute of me to offer. She glanced at Jordan as if to ask him why in the world he brought me there, but all he did was shake her off before sitting me up on the counter and pulling me into a kiss. I didn't know what the big deal was with offering to help, but Bev always looked at me funny after that.

Now that Jordan dumped me, I'm sure someone like Bev would probably stop looking at me altogether. But that shouldn't stop me from going to her parties.

It's been a week since I yelled at Cameron at the lake and I've done a scarily good job of avoiding him at school. It hasn't been that hard since I'm basically a social pariah now that everyone knows about my breakup with Jordan. My seat at the popular table has become suddenly unavailable, as I imagined, and I spend most lunches eating in the auditorium or in the back of Blaze's car when she isn't running around school for all the other clubs she's involved in.

She and I still haven't talked about Cameron, or the fact that she's been lying to me. My feelings are hurt, but I keep trying to remember that Blaze has never lied to me before. If she's doing it now, she must have a good reason for it. But that doesn't make it suck any less.

There are only a few soccer games left of the Fall season, so my teammates are being nice to me if only for the fact they want me to stay focused on scoring goals. Jordan won't be coming to any of my games, that much was obvious. My only hope is that it doesn't affect the turnout and our coach's morale. Or change his mind about making me captain next year. After everything that's happened, I don't want to lose soccer. It seems to be the one good thing I have going for me these days.

My mom walks in and knocks on the door while she enters the room, interrupting my busy thoughts. I hate when she does that. Why bother knocking in the first place if you're going to walk in? She's in a deep blue tracksuit and I can tell she came from a run even though there isn't a drop of sweat on her body. Not sure how that happens.

"Going out tonight, girls?" she asks us, her voice rising an octave in excitement.

"Yeah, there's a party at Bev's," I respond. I walk over to my closet to see if I can match up a pair of ripped jeans with some sort of cute shirt that will make me look somewhat presentable. No luck. I really need to take my mom up on that shopping trip soon.

"The party of the year," my mom chuckles. "Do you want to borrow something?"

I hesitate as I put the hanger holding the shirt in my hands back onto the rack in the closet. My mom isn't much taller than I am, so we're usually around the same size. I used to borrow her dresses for church all the time, they were always so much cuter than what was in my closet. A lawyer's wardrobe is nothing to fawn over, but a woman who's a lawyer has a different level of taste.

Blaze's eyebrows shoot up at the possibility of going into my mom's closet. A rare experience, for sure.

"Really? You mean it?" I ask her.

Her face lights up as she walks out of my room and down the stairs to her own. Blaze and I follow her and I realize this is the first time she's ever even seen my mom's room. It looks the same to me, wall to ceiling with ocean-themed decor. For a moment I'm grateful she hasn't changed anything since Dad died. Since he was the one who wanted the ocean theme, it feels like part of him is still here when looking around the room.

The lamp on the bedside table is a seahorse, the comforter on her bed light blue and covered in a sand dollar print. Our school could have probably used everything in here for the homecoming dance without spending a dime on other decorations. She even has one of those wall plug-ins by the door that poof out a smell every hour. It smells like the beach, which I love, but this one is a little too sunscreen-y for my taste.

Everything is doubled in size of what I assume would be average for any other house. Her bedroom is massive, and her bathroom could fit two entire smaller bedrooms in it itself. She leads us back into her closet, which is probably a mile long, every inch filled with different kinds of dresses. From casual to chic, all the way to fancy pantsuits. There are sparkles and glossy items and I'm not sure what is catching my eye first. I recognize some of the dresses from days she went to court, and others I assume were for dates. Dates with my dad. Dates she'll never have again.

My mom isn't the only lawyer in town, but she's treated as if she is. Being Board Certified in a few different areas of law makes her the go-to person for the small town woes of car accidents, divorces, even environmental protection. She's a superstar, even though she was never really around for most of my childhood. My dad stayed home with me and Jenna, while my mom worked to give us a life she was proud of.

After he died, she went right back to work. I had hoped she would take more time to be here for me, for Jenna, for herself, but that wasn't the case. Her job has always been her life, but I didn't know how much that bothered me until now. As if losing one parent isn't hard enough.

I walk down the closet and admire the fabric of the dresses in the back. Jenna and I used to come in here when we were younger and play dress up. We played 'wedding' so many times, our dad would make fun of us for not knowing the right way to walk down the fake aisle that we would create out of old towels and blankets.

My throat clenches as I realize he'll never get to see that day for either of us. I know Jenna probably doesn't care, but my wedding has always been something I dreamed about. I want a beach wedding, but I also want to do all of the typical rituals—the first-look, the father-daughter dance, the giving away of the bride. I could easily picture my dad hiding his tears as I turned around in my long, flowy white dress and me telling him to stop crying or he would make me start and I would ruin my makeup. He would laugh and tell me that I was beautiful, with or without makeup. This was something he was always telling me as I started experimenting in my early teenage years. My poor pillow and the dozens of makeup wipes I went through during my eyeliner phase agree with him.

We would have had to take classes before our big dance, otherwise he would do everything in his power to embarrass me with his outdated disco moves. Secretly, I would love it and hope someone caught it on camera so I could laugh at it in ten years. I could see him walking me down the sandy beach to meet the love of my life, whoever that may be. He would be crying, again, and I would be shaking. I would squeeze his hand and tell him not to let me go, like I did when I was four and he took off my bicycle training wheels. Same as he did then, he would look me in the eye and tell me "It's time, Lexie." I could picture it so easily, it hurt. My picture is going to have to change now and I hate that.

"Wear whatever you'd like." My mom interrupts my thoughts. "Some of these I've never even worn, and probably still have the tags on, but that's fine, you can rip them off."

Blaze's mouth forms a perfectly shaped 'O' as she makes her way through the clothes.

I find a slim red mini dress somewhere in the middle of the rack, and I hold it up to myself while looking in the mirror. Lawyers loved wearing tight dresses.

Perfect, I think. It's hot enough for the party and sexy enough to make Cameron's jaw drop. The thought surprises me and I try to shake my head, shove away any thoughts about him. I doubt Cameron would even be at this party, and I shouldn't be looking to impress him even if he is there. I'm still mad at him, but for some reason I can't stop thinking about him either. Which is exactly what I need.

I grab a pair of black strappy heels on my way out of my mom's closet and head upstairs with Blaze to finish getting ready.

****

We walk up to the front door of Bev's house and my head immediately starts to *thrum* at the booms of the bass coming from inside. I physically have to hold my breath as I walk in the front door. *God*, I forgot how much of a stoner Bev's brother was. Even when he isn't around, the house always reeks of pot.

There are string lights draped over the doorway and some more are scattered across the long granite countertop of the kitchen island. The party started an hour ago, but there are already plastic cups and empty beer cans lying on the floor. Music is *thumping* from the massive speakers in the living room and people are scattered all about, from the kitchen to the backyard. Bev's house is probably the biggest I'd ever seen, three stories including a basement.

Like my mom said, it's the party of the year. And it looks like the entire school is here.

Blaze and I make our way downstairs to the basement, the usual hangout for the popular crowd. I guess we really don't belong down here anymore, but it's a force of habit at this point. Once we climb down, my eyes find Jordan almost immediately. I've been so used to always seeking him out at parties like this for so many months, it's hard to turn that part of myself off. Old habits and all that.

He's sitting on the large orange sofa—a classic staple of the basement—and I try not to think about the last time I was in this house on that same sofa with him. Now, there's a girl next to him that I don't recognize. She looks short, with blonde hair shaped into a pixie cut above her ears. Even from where I'm standing, I can see the piercings that go all the way up her ear. Jordan laughs and brushes a strand of hair from her forehead when his gaze meets mine and the whites of his eyes stand out so brightly in shock I think I might faint.

He jumps up from his spot on the couch and walks over to where Blaze and I are standing. *Oh, no.* This is not happening.

He's spent the last two weeks ignoring me, acting as if I never even existed. Whenever I saw him around school, he was either laughing with the football team or shoving his tongue so far down Paige's throat I swore he was going to get it stuck there. He is *not* walking over to approach me now.

I turn around so fast that I smack right into a couple making out at the edge of the staircase. They weren't there a moment before, and my eyes blink to assure myself that they're real.

"Mind it, would ya?" The girl snaps at me before returning her tongue to the guy's mouth.

Yep, they're real.

The last thing I want to do is have a front row seat to a spit swapping fest tonight. I turn back around and start to make my way back up the stairs when I find myself face to face with Jordan. Suddenly my throat feels dry and on fire at the same time. I haven't talked to him since homecoming. He got a haircut, I notice. His short brown hair is shaven in a light buzz cut. *He looks good* and my attraction to him pisses me off.

"Lexi, damn, babe," he stutters and slurs his words.

Great. Not only is he here, but he's drunk. I always hated the way Jordan was when he was drunk. His ego shot up by a thousand and his hands got ten times more grabby. I remember the night of the bonfire and suddenly feel the need to be sick when I haven't even had anything to drink yet.

"Hi and bye." I try to push past him, but he doesn't let me go around him.

"Wait, wait, what's the rush? It's good to see you. I mean I know you come to Bev's parties, but I didn't think you would anymore," he says.

Okay, that pisses me off. Because he broke up with me means I'm not allowed to go to parties? It's only been two weeks since he dumped me. It's not like it's been years.

"Why, because I'm a virgin? Because I won't give it up so why bother coming to a party in the first place?" I spit at him.

He blinks as if he doesn't understand a word I said and then smiles. I used to love his smile, the way his dimples were always uneven and how his back crooked tooth always became visible. Now his dimples make me nauseated and I want to punch that stupid crooked tooth right out of his mouth.

"Lexi, baby, has anyone here told you what a smoke show you are? Like damn, look at that dress. I don't remember ever seeing that dress before." He starts to come closer to me, his hand feeling like ice as it rests on the familiar spot on my back.

"Why don't we go upstairs and talk, huh? Things ended on such a bad note, I don't want it to be like that," he adds.

My heart clenches at the thought of being near him again, my body reflexively leaning into his touch as his hand moves further down my back. My mind is screaming at me to turn around, to walk out of this house right now, and not look back. It's been almost two weeks and now he wants to talk? Do I really want to listen to him?

Part of me is curious to hear what he has to say. Another part of me wants to knee him in the groin for what he did. I'm not sure which part wins myself over, but I make up my mind and nod at Jordan to lead the way.

"Are you sure you're okay?" Blaze asks me, and I realize how she's been standing there the whole time, witnessing my run in with Jordan.

"I'll be fine, Blaze. I'll find you in a bit," I say to her and look back at Jordan, raising my one eyebrow to note my impatience.

His smile grows and he takes my hand to pull us up the basement staircase and then up another set of wooden stairs to the second story of Bev's house. We had been to at least two parties here together, and we even had a specific bedroom we would use to make out in. Jordan clearly knows this and I try to hold back my laughter as he opens the door to the familiar bedroom on the far-right of the house. But I'm overcome with confusion when I see the once pink room is now painted a faint mint green.

"Whoa, what happened here?" I ask as I look around.

The two double beds are gone and replaced by a gigantic king panel, a green comforter matching the color of the light textured walls. The bay window that was once filled with stuffed animals and toys now held elegant-looking pillows and a couple of academic textbooks.

"I guess they decided to redecorate, who cares. Come here," Jordan states as he turns me around to face him.

He places his hand on the side of my face and I close my eyes. I can't even remember how many times the last few days I've thought of him holding me like this, of being back in his arms as if I never left. Maybe it took being without him to realize how much I miss him. But for some reason, it doesn't feel as amazing as I imagined it would have.

"It looks so different," I complain as I relax with him. Does he not care that our room doesn't even look like our room anymore?

"You look so hot tonight. I missed you so much." He leans and presses his lips behind my ear. A shiver runs down my arms at the feeling of his breath on my skin.

I push him back and say, "I thought you wanted to talk."

He smirks and steps closer again. "I do, baby, but first let me hold you." He pouts and I give in.

This all feels so normal, being at Bev's party, in Jordan's arms. But something about it doesn't feel normal at all, and not only because our room looks entirely different than it had a few months ago.

"Now tell me, why didn't you ever wear this dress for me?" He places his finger under my chin to bring my gaze up to his. Again, I'm reminded of all the ways Jordan tried to claim me and make me his own. "Maybe if you dressed like this more, I wouldn't have gotten so distracted."

Two weeks later and that's the best he can come up with? And now the breakup is my fault because I didn't dress how he wanted me to? The part of me from a moment ago that wanted to knee him in the groin is brought back to life. I'm about to do it when his next sentence holds me in place.

"I was wrong—for what happened with Paige. I never should have let her get in the way of us. I'm so sorry, baby." He bites his lower lip. Despite my best efforts, nerves fill my stomach.

He looks down from my eyes to my lips, then back up to my eyes. Every bone in my body is reacting to his gaze even though I don't want them to. His lips brush mine softly, and all of a sudden the familiar feeling of safety and comfort rushes through me. I part my mouth to taste more of him as his hands find my hair. He spins me around and pins me against the back of the door, pressing his lips further into my own and letting his tongue find mine. He tastes like cheap beer and raspberry ChapStick. My stomach is swirling now, filling with nausea and excitement at the same time.

His hands are everywhere, moving from the back of my neck and down my back. I can't catch up to what is happening, I can't comprehend that I'm back here, in this room, in Jordan's arms. He's whispering between kisses, saying how much he missed my body, how he can't wait to be with me for real this time, and how he made such a mistake by letting me get away. My body goes rigid as his hand slides under my dress. This cannot be happening again.

"Jordan, stop." I start to push him off and he listens, which is surprising. "This is too fast, we're supposed to be talking," I add as I pull my dress back down to an appropriate length.

"We are talking, baby, we're us again. That's what you wanted, right?" He tries to kiss me again, but I duck out from underneath his barricade against the door.

I catch myself looking around the room again, not finding a single thing that used to be here before. He must understand what I'm doing because he comes up from behind me and wraps his arms around my waist. I used to love when he held me like this, but now I'm not so sure it feels the same.

"It's okay, Lex, it's a room. Things change." He rests his chin on my shoulder.

It's that moment that brings me back to reality, and I realize my body isn't warming to his touch, my heart no longer racing when he says my name.

He's not my Jordan anymore and we will never be "us" again.

He's right, things change. Things changed with us, and it's all his fault.

"Exactly," I say as a turn to face him. "Things change, Jordan. People change. Circumstances change. Everything between us has changed. You broke my heart with Paige that night. You threw away everything because I wouldn't give it up according to your timeline. And then you go and cheat on me with someone who is supposed to be my friend!" I start to get louder and he shrinks uncomfortably.

"Whoa, Lex, let's chill, all right. If you don't want to hook up that's cool, I'll leave," he says as if there is nothing wrong with the fact and starts to head towards the door. Is he for real?

Suddenly, I remember the girl with the pixie-cut he was flirting with before he saw me. He's probably trying to determine if he still has time to catch up with her. And where the hell is Paige? I cannot believe him.

Laughter pours out of me so quickly I can't suppress it. Jordan looks at me in complete confusion as I continue to crack up. My hand grips the bottom of my stomach and I lean over the foot of the bed, laughing so hard that I can't breathe. He will never change. I can't believe I almost let my guard down with him even for a second.

"Fine, Jordan, leave. You're good at that." I start and realize how little I actually care about being in the same room as him. "I can't believe I wasted so many months on you, doing every little thing for you to try to keep your eyes on me. Even more, I can't believe I wasted so many tears over you. Thinking over what I did wrong, how I could have prevented you hooking up with Paige. But that was my mistake," I clip at him as I realize something. The thought is overwhelming, but I can't escape the truth that comes with it.

"Paige was right. You were a distraction, Jordan," I continue as the realization hits me like a pile of bricks. "I thought that if I spent all my time with you and your little group, I wouldn't think about my dad anymore. That you would make me happy enough to get over his death. But I was wrong, and you know what? It wasn't fair of me to put that expectation on you or our relationship."

He rolls his eyes as if my presence alone is one giant inconvenience.

"We're not *us* again, Jordan. We aren't anything. So honestly, thank you. Thank you for ripping out my heart before I could even give it to you fully in the first place. You made the right call with Paige," I realize as he raises his eyebrows.

He opens his mouth to speak, but I hold up my hand to cut him off.

"Don't," I spit out. "I don't know what happened between you and her, and frankly, I really don't care. But that girl out there that you seem to be toying with? She deserves better. My advice? Try something new. Do something good for a change."

I spin on my heels and walk out of the bedroom, back down the stairs to the main floor. My chest is already tightening and the way this dress is clinging to me is not helping. The back of my throat feels dry and my vision starts to blur, the tears ready and waiting.

Not here, I push them back. Not yet.

On the main floor, I scan the room for Blaze, but there are too many people milling about. The last thing I want to do is go back down to the basement. My only freedom is the front door, which I rush out of hastily. The fresh air is a cool reassurance against my warm skin. My hands frantically type into my phone, texting Blaze I'm ready to go.

My cheek feels wet, and I reach a hand up to catch the culprit tear in action. *No, no*, give me a few more minutes. The entire school doesn't need to see me become a blubbering mess.

A few minutes later Blaze finds me on the front porch and we get into her car to go back to my house. As soon as the doors shut, my body reacts.

A tsunami runs down my face and I bury myself into the palms of my hands.

"Alex?" Blaze reaches over in concern. I can't answer her, I can't do anything to stop it.

The tsunami is turning into an avalanche, every cell in my body breaking apart.

"Let's get you home." I hear the click of her seatbelt and the motion of the car moving forward. The drive to my house is silent, save for my breath hitching and the sobs that are finally beginning to calm down.

"Do I even want to know what happened?" Blaze asks when she parks in my driveway.

My breath starts to even out, enough that I can speak. I briefly tell her about Jordan trying to get back together with me and don't skip over the part where he pushed for more—yet again.

"What a piece of shit." She shakes her head at me.

Through my tears, a laugh comes out of my mouth. Blaze almost never curses and the word sounds foreign coming out of her mouth.

"Stop!" She hits my arm playfully. "He really is one."

"You're right, but it was funny hearing you say that. Thank you, I needed a laugh."

Once my vision clears, my brain does at almost the same time. The next admission is going to do me in.

"Paige and Cameron were right about me," I sigh and lean my head against the car window. All of the realizations of the night are hitting me in the face again.

Blaze stares at me questioningly, so I tell her about Paige saying I never loved Jordan, that I was using him as a distraction, expanding on the outburst Blaze witnessed at the diner a few weeks ago.

My chest starts to lighten, and I know what I have to admit despite how wrong it feels.

"I've been so angry," I say. "For the last six months, everyone has made me feel like an idiot for being upset about my dad dying. It feels like I'm going crazy."

"I didn't—" she starts to say.

"I know, but you have." I give her a comforting look to let her know I'm not mad.

"What did Cameron say about you?" she asks.

This is another conversation I need to have with her. I only hope it goes the way I want it to.

"Blaze, why did you lie to me about him?" I ask her.

Confusion spreads across her face, and she doesn't know what to say.

"He told me you guys talk, that you invited him to the club that night. I know you know him." I look at her with a sad smile, again to let her know I'm not mad. Which is true, I'm not mad. I'm confused.

"I've known him forever," she blows out a long breath. "His dad is really good friends with my parents, so he was kind of always around."

"Did you guys…" I try to find the words. "Did you ever…"

Her eyes widen in shock as she realizes what I'm

trying to say. Thank goodness, because I don't know if I would have even been able to say it.

"Oh, god, no! Ew, gross!" She shakes her head at the thought. "It was never like that. He was like a brother to me. A really annoying older brother," she laughs. I let out a chuckle of my own. Yep, that sounds like Cameron.

"How come he and I never met?" I ask next. It's not like I haven't practically lived at Blaze's house growing up, and vice versa.

"I don't know," she shrugs. "I guess I never really thought about it. You were my best friend, and he was someone who was always around when his parents were over. It didn't ever occur to me to mix the two."

My eyebrows lift. "Until it did."

"I tried to be there for him when his mom died—oh crap, did he tell you about that?" she blushes. I nod my head and she breathes a sigh of relief at not giving away one of his secrets. "He started pushing me away after that. He still came over, but for the most part we sat in silence or he went in another room to play video games until it was time for him to leave. We only started talking again a few months ago. He knew who you were, but he was always asking me about you."

My heart flutters at the idea of Cameron asking about me. Maybe he does feel the same way I do.

"I couldn't tell if he had a crush on you or if he wanted to help you. You know, because of your dad—"

I wave my hand at her and nod my head to cut her off. She doesn't need to finish that sentence. We both know how it ends.

"When I invited him to the club, I had no idea you guys were getting so close. Honestly." She stares at me so intently I know she's trying to let me know she's telling the truth. I believe her. She's still my best friend, and has no reason to lie to me.

"I thought he would come hang out with us, have a good time. I know you had me, but I thought he would be a good friend to you. Maybe make you feel better about the whole Paige and Jordan thing. Which he did, apparently *too* well." She winks at me.

"Stop it," I laugh and swat her arm.

"But I'm serious, I didn't know you were into each other like that. Which is my bad for being totally oblivious to the obvious." She rolls her eyes.

It makes sense now, why she didn't tell me she knew it was Cameron in the club that night. She was embarrassed. She was trying to be a good friend, trying to make me feel better. She had no idea Cameron would kiss me, or that I was actually starting to have real feelings for him. And that's my fault, I haven't told her. I've been so used to holding everything in, I forgot what was *normal* to share with other people.

"That's my fault, I didn't tell you. But to be fair, I didn't really know that I was that into him either," I laugh. "He was right about me, too, though."

"What do you mean?" Blaze asks.

"It didn't make sense to me before, but something about the whole thing that happened with Jordan tonight made me understand." I glance out the windshield and hope my mom doesn't come rushing out the front door to get us inside yet.

"Cameron said what I was doing wasn't going to bring my dad back. He thinks I was dating Jordan and hanging out with the other girls to avoid the reality of him being gone."

"Like a distraction." Blaze catches on and I nod to her.

"I think they're both right. Cameron and Paige, I mean. Here I am pissed off at Paige for backstabbing me and hurt over Jordan breaking my heart. But in reality, I was using Jordan and the popularity as a distraction. Not intentionally, but that's what happened. God, I'm a horrible person."

"You're not a horrible person."

"But think about it, Blaze. I've been selfish, manipulative, and careless. What does that say about me?"

"It says you're human." Blaze touches my arm, the sympathy in her eyes and in her tone overwhelming me.

The intimacy of her touch and the intense moment get the better of me and suddenly the tears are flowing down my face again before I can stop them.

"I-I'm sorry," I stutter and try to calm myself down.

She reaches over the center console and engulfs me in her arms. I can't remember the last time someone held me like this, really held me, and it feels too good to break off. The tears are coming faster now and after a moment, the tsunami returns. If it was anyone else, I would be embarrassed by my breakdown. But thankfully, it's Blaze.

"I'm so sorry, Lex. I thought I was helping," she starts. "I've never lost anyone like you have, I didn't know what to do. You would talk about how your mom seemed fine, how your sister seemed fine. I thought that was normal, and I wanted to help you be okay."

"It's not your fault," I assure her. Because it isn't, it isn't anyone's fault.

I'm the one in control of my actions, my reactions, my emotions. I'm the one who isn't dealing with them the way I should be. Another thing that Cameron said enters my mind and I realize what bothered me so much about it when I walked away that day at the lake.

He said I needed to process my grief. That if I didn't, it would make everything worse. He was right about that, too. I haven't been processing anything, I've been avoiding it.

And it's finally catching up to me. Two tsunamis and an avalanche later.

"My dad died," I say in between sobs. "He *died*, and my sister left. How is any of that normal? How can anyone go on like something that big never happened? I've tried. For six months, I've tried to move on. At the funeral, my mom told me to do whatever I needed to find a way to 'get over it'," I repeat her words. "It was so easy for her! For Jenna! They both picked up and moved on with their lives. As if he didn't even exist. As if his death doesn't even matter."

Snaps and breaks come from inside my chest, my heart shattering into a million pieces. My sobs break apart, but come back with a force so strong that no sound physically escapes my lips.

Every bone in my body aches. My head throbs so loudly I can't think straight.

Someone throws a baseball at my stomach, but it's stuck there, driving deeper and deeper into my gut.

My mom still hasn't come outside and I'm grateful. The conversation I need to have with her is going to send me over the edge and I'm not ready for that yet. I don't know when she turns the car off and gets out of her seat, but the next thing I know, my door is open and Blaze is gathering me in her arms from my position in the car.

"Shh... it's okay, Lex. It's okay. Breathe, try to breathe," she soothes me. "I want you to find something to look at and stare at it. Concentrate on that object and take a few deep breaths."

My body leans into her, my eyes trying to focus

on something besides the darkness encompassing my mind. With the way she's holding me, her right arm is wrapped around the front of my body. I clutch to it, feeling a light piece of string on her wrist. It's a bracelet, loose threads intertwined together and hanging low off her arm. There's a pink string, a yellow one, and a green. I focus on the colors and how they loop together as I try to breathe.

"He mattered, Alex. He will always matter." I hear her say as I close my eyes, tempted to succumb to the black clouds spiraling all around me. Focusing on the colors of her bracelet to keep me from going under.

Pink, yellow, green. Pink, yellow, green.

All of a sudden the colors start to change in the back of my mind. New hues and layers taking over.

Pale blue, flakes of emerald.

The depths of the ocean. With a hint of devastation.

Chapter Fourteen

Somehow, I make it inside.

Blaze's arm is clutching my own, her grip so strong she's probably scared I will fall without her. She'd be right.

The soft fabric of the couch settles underneath me as she sits me down. The last few minutes are coming back to me now that my body has decided to calm itself. Cameron's eyes are still burning in the back of my mind. Glancing around the room centers me, I'm in the living room. The large oak coffee table sits before me. There's noises coming from the kitchen, my mom rifling through drawers and cabinets.

"Are you going to be okay?" Blaze asks me.

I stare back at my emo goddess of a best friend, unsure of what I would do without her. Who I would *be* without her. The vague memory of my breakdown enters my thoughts and I feel guilty she had to deal with that. She had to deal with *me*.

"I'll be fine, Blaze. You really should go home, you've done more than enough for me tonight," I tell her.

She stares at me for a moment, trying to find the uncertainty in my voice. But there is none. I mean it. She's done way too much for me.

Besides, the conversation I'm about to have is long overdue, and she doesn't need to be here for it. She hugs me quickly before scurrying out the door, her absence immediately making my heart clench. My phone *pings* and startles me from my blank state on the couch.

I'll be there in ten minutes the text from my sister reads.

After my breakdown, Blaze called my sister and told her to come home. I could hear Jenna questioning my best friend over the phone, but Blaze was persistent.

Two hours later and my sister would be here any minute. My mom is still in the kitchen, the strong scent of jasmine tea filling the air around me. She's called out to me a few times, but I don't answer. I want to wait for Jenna to get here.

The small amount of confidence I gained after completely falling apart in Blaze's car is diminishing and I'm trying not to lose my nerve. Something happened tonight.

Something changed.

The overwhelming realization about avoiding my grief sent me into a spiral and I need to talk to my family. I need them to know how I feel, what the past six months have been like for me. One last failed attempt to see if I'm alone in all of this. It's so obvious now.

And Cameron saw it from the very beginning.

Moments later, the front door swings open and my sister comes into view. I haven't seen her in months, but she's still as beautiful as the last time. Her long brown hair, a twin color to my own, shines brighter. *She must have gotten highlights*, I think to myself. It hangs low over her shoulders and curls deeply in a way I can never get mine to do. She's in a strapless maxi sundress, with a white jean jacket resting on her arm, her white Tory Burch sandals sticking out against her tan skin.

She looks nice, and I realize I might have interrupted her evening. I feel a little bad about that, but this is too important. Hopefully she won't hold it against me.

My mom briefly kisses her on the cheek before handing her a cup of tea. I watch as Jenna kicks off her sandals, sets her jacket down on the end table, and comes to sit next to me on the couch. Mom follows, handing me the other mug in her hand. The black tea is piping hot, steam flowing into my face heavily. It feels wonderful on my puffy face, which Jenna is staring at incredulously now.

I take a small sip of the tea, careful not to burn my tongue on the scalding liquid. My throat is soothed immediately by the warmth of the drink.

"Okay, what happened? When Blaze said it was an emergency, I thought something happened to you." My sister looks at me carefully.

Her eyes rake over my body, as if she's assessing if I've broken any bones or have other physical features out of place.

"Is this about your breakup with Jordan?" My mom looks at me.

"You and Jordan broke up? When? Why?" Jenna presses.

"Yes, we broke up but no, this isn't about that," I tell them both. "This is about Dad," I take a deep breath before I continue. "And before either of you say anything, you are going to let me talk. You are going to listen to me."

The authority in my tone catches me by surprise, but I try not to let it falter my motivation. I take their silence as agreement to my condition and muster up whatever confidence I have left to press on. Here goes nothing.

Actually, here goes *everything*.

"Dad died. He's dead, and he's not coming back. You two acted like his death didn't even happen. Or worse, like it did happen, but that it was such a miniscule interruption to your lives that you shook off and moved on from." I point at Jenna. "*You* didn't even come to the funeral."

Jenna moves to open her mouth, but I hold my hand up, letting her know I'm not finished.

"I'm seventeen years old. To some people, I'm practically considered an adult. To me, I'm still that—a seventeen-year-old girl. I lost my *father*, not my favorite pair of earrings. He was a real person, he was *our* person, and he died." My breath catches, but I push forward. "I needed you. I *needed* you, and you weren't there. It was like you left me, too," I choke out the last part and realize I'm crying again.

God, I'm so tired of having water leak out of my eyes.

"I guess I'm not normal, because I can't wake up and act like none of this ever happened. I tried, I really did. But it didn't work, and now I have all of this horrible darkness inside of me trying to get out and it hurts. It all hurts so much." I'm sobbing harder now, and I reach forward to set my mug down on the coffee table in front of the couch.

Jenna pulls me into her arms and looks at me questioningly, as if she's asking if I'm finished talking. I nod my head, my body feeling weak from how much energy it takes to complete the simple motion. Exhaustion is taking over. I'm not sure how much longer I can hold my head up.

"Alex, I didn't come to the funeral because I couldn't. I couldn't see him in that way—lying there all cold and pale. I couldn't handle all the people coming up to me and saying they were sorry, that I was in their prayers. I knew Mom would be there, that she would be there for you. I don't know why, but I couldn't face you that day. It was too hard." She sniffles and I look up to see her wiping a few stray tears away from her face. "I honestly thought it would be better for you if I wasn't there. I thought you would be able to grieve him yourself without having me there to influence your emotions. I thought I was helping you."

"You never even want to talk about him," I accuse her. "Every time I bring him up, you get so angry. You get so mean."

"I-I'm sorry," she shrugs. "Talking about him hurts. The moment I do, I lose it."

Her words tumble around in my head, trying to make sense. I lose it too, but in a completely different way.

"But we *need* to talk about him, don't you see that? Otherwise it's going to hurt like this forever."

"I'm sorry," she whispers.

"And I thought I was helping by being strong for you," my mom chimes in and I glance over at her now. "I loved your father, and I especially loved how much he cared for both of you girls. I wanted you to see that you still had someone in your life that was here for you, that cared about you."

I shake my head, unable to understand her logic here.

She folds her hands together and I notice for the first time how bad they're trembling. "I wanted to be that person, and I couldn't do that if I let myself break around you. So, yes, I went back to work. It was the only thing I knew how to do. And yes, I shrugged it all off when we were together because I thought that was the only way. But don't think for a second that I haven't been bawling my eyes out behind closed doors."

A piece of me breaks at the thought of my mom crying alone, with no one to comfort her. She didn't just lose her children's father, she also lost the love of her life.

"I wouldn't have thought less of you if you weren't strong," I say to her. "I watched both of you pick yourselves back up and move on, without even falling down in the first place. I felt like I was constantly falling, but because no one else was, I wasn't allowed to. So it left me in this weird state of limbo with all sorts of conflicting feelings."

I think about riding the Tower of Terror with my dad years ago, that gut-wrenching feeling in my stomach from plummeting down, down, down. How it feels like I've been feeling that same sensation for the last six months. How it never seems to leave me.

"I needed both of you." I tighten my hold on Jenna's waist. "I still do."

It's silent for what feels like a good five minutes before my sister pushes me out of her lap and places her hand on the side of my cheek.

"I'm so sorry, Alex. We didn't want you to see us fall. We thought it would be better if you didn't see us break. But we were wrong, and we see that now," she says to me.

"I think maybe," my mom smiles sadly and walks over to sit in between me and my sister. She puts her arms around the both of us and brings us into a tight hug. "We were all supposed to fall together so that we could help build each other back up, one piece at a time."

It's at that moment, where we're all sitting there weeping and holding each other, that I realize how wrong I've been. I'm not alone.

My mom and sister are as upset about my dad dying as I am. They're grieving, too, in their own way. It's not my place to question that, to expect their grieving process to be the same as my own. We all lost the same person, but how we deal with that loss is completely up to us.

They don't teach you that in school—how to grieve. They teach you how to tie your shoes, and then you learn some math problems, and even how to write in cursive, which I'm still not sure is entirely necessary. But they don't teach you what to do when you lose someone you love. Someone who was a huge part of your life.

They don't tell you how long to cry for or how long to be angry for. We don't have funeral rehearsals to practice what we want to say or what to put on a headstone. We don't learn how to prepare for those sympathy responses we all come to hate at some point.

We all have to figure it out for ourselves, one step at a time. *I* am trying to figure it out for myself, one step at a time. And I'm thankful I don't have to do it alone.

****

"It looks so bland," Jenna says.

"Those flowers still look nice," comes from my mom.

We're sitting on the big, concrete stone bench at the cemetery, looking over my dad's grave. The ants are not present today, thank God, and that probably has something to do with the rain that's trickling down onto us. The large oak tree above us shields us well and the added bonus of our umbrellas keeps us dry from the falling water dripping off of the leaves.

Last night was filled with lots of tears and hugs. Eventually, we all fell asleep in my mom's bedroom. Despite our long conversations, my stomach still felt uneasy when I woke up this morning. Like there's still something missing. But I have no idea what it is.

Jenna is the one who suggested we come here today. I smiled from ear to ear when she woke up and immediately asked if we could all go see Dad together. A round of showers and a half-hour drive later, we pulled up to the cemetery. I remember the walk to my dad's grave immediately, even though I haven't been here in months. Not since that one and only time.

It looks the same, only the grass was fully set now and growing wildly across the lawn. The headstone is duller, not as shiny and new as when I first saw it. But my fake flowers are still in the ceramic vase at the center of the headstone—the reds and yellows of the rhododendrons still as vibrant and lively as when I first placed them there. Fake flowers were definitely a smart choice.

"Our names are on it, see Jenna? There," I say and point to the engraving under our father's name.

"He loved you girls. He loved you both so much," my mom says under her breath, sniffling back a few tears.

I have a feeling we're going to be crying a lot for the next few months. But at least we will be doing it together.

"I don't know if I'm ever going to stop missing him," I say, shocking myself at verbalizing the truth for once. This not holding back thing already feels so good.

My mom puts her hand on my shoulder. "You won't, but that's okay. No one expects you to stop missing him, sweetie."

"I'm going to miss him for the rest of my life." Jenna's smile is small as she stares at her feet.

"I remember the day we brought you home, Jenna," my mom takes a breath. "You were so beautiful. This tiny little thing... I had never seen anything so fragile. Your dad and I were over the moon. But your dad, he was also terrified. He didn't take his eyes off you in your cradle. Wherever you went, he went too. He couldn't leave your side."

My heart twinges at the story, both out of love for Jenna and jealousy for myself. Jealousy isn't a good look on me, but I want a memory about dad, too.

"When I got pregnant again, with you," my mom nudges me with her arm. "I was so excited—two baby girls for me to spoil and love."

I can't help it, my eyes roll at her cheesiness.

"I was nervous, worried you two would grow up hating each other instead of being friends."

Jenna and I both stare at her now, unaware of the thought even being an option. Jenna's my sister, I can't imagine ever hating her.

"Anyway, I was talking with your dad one night and I had mentioned at one point how I hoped you two would stick together as you grew up, that you wouldn't let petty differences and unwarranted anger get between you."

Again Jenna and I glance at each other, knowing something like that could never happen. No matter what tries to come between us.

"Your dad was in the kitchen at the time and I heard him laugh so loud it filled the entire house."

For a moment, I can almost hear his laugh in the distance. It's always been my favorite sound.

"He came over and said to me, 'Sara, that will never happen. These girls are resilient, they are fighters. Look at the people who made them.'"

"Ew, gross." Jenna sticks out her tongue at my mom's words.

"Oh, stop it," she swats her leg playfully. "He said 'Even if they grow up to hate each other, or they take years to reconnect, they will always have each other. God forbid anything happens to one of us, the girls will never be alone. They will always have each other to lean on.'"

Her words make me smile and Jenna starts to whimper again. I wrap my arm around her shoulder and pull her into my chest.

"I'm so sorry, Alex. God, I'm so sorry."

"What? Jenna, what are you apologizing for?" I question her.

"Dad's one and only wish for having you, for giving me one of the best gifts I could ever ask for was for us to be there for each other. And I haven't been doing that. I've failed you. I failed Dad," she sobs harder and a few tears of my own escape from the corner of my eyes.

"Oh, Jenna, no. You haven't failed me. And you have definitely not failed Dad," I assure her. "You're my sister, Jenna. You're my favorite person, even when we don't get along. Even when you piss me off, or you make fun of me for not knowing what an Alpha Data Pie is."

That gets me the reaction I'm looking for. Jenna starts laughing and swats at my arm.

"It's Alpha *Zeta* Pi, dummy."

"See? What would I do without you?"

She rolls her eyes at me, but tightens her hold around my arms. I hug her again, gently kissing the top of her head. My mom is smiling at us and I place a hand on her arm to acknowledge her before going back to hugging my sister. My gorgeous sister, who I've missed so much.

"It's you and me forever, Jen. Like Dad said. As long as we have each other, we will never be alone." I smile through her hair.

She stares up at the sky and I watch as she closes her eyes and takes a deep breath.

"Do you think he's here? Watching us?" she asks.

I think about her words for a moment, taking in the space around us. The cemetery grounds, headstones and flowers stretching on for miles. Tree branches swaying above our heads, squirrels chasing each other through the leaves. Sounds of the raindrops *pitter-pattering* on the top of our umbrellas.

I close my own eyes, tilting my head back towards the sky, mimicking her position.

"I think so." I squeeze her hand. "I think he's always here."

****

"Alex! Breakfast is ready!" I hear my mom scream as I finish tying my hair up into a ponytail. The smell of crispy bacon reaches all the way to my bathroom, a growl coming from my stomach in response.

"Coming!" I yell back. I head downstairs and am overwhelmed by the scent of the bacon with an added smell of chocolate chip pancakes. *Mm*, my favorite.

"Well, excuse me! I didn't know breakfast was fancy today," my sister laughs and spins me around to admire my outfit.

I blush and take a seat at the dining room table. *I do look good today*, I think.

An oversized white sweater covers me and is tucked into a black leather skirt with thin tights underneath and a pair of black ankle booties. It's cute, and it's not something I typically wear. But now it feels like me. Or a new version of me, at least.

Jenna ended up staying the whole weekend, and besides visiting Dad's grave, we spent almost half of our nights staying up and talking with my mom. We cried, we laughed, and even shared a few memories about Dad. It was awkward, but it also felt right at the same time. It was exactly what the three of us needed. What *I* needed.

As my mom fills our coffee cups and goes to place the pot back in the kitchen, I can't help but smile at how much has changed over the last couple of nights. I also can't help but smile at the hope for what's to come.

"Oh, my goodness, Mom, your chocolate chip pancakes put every other diner in Summersville to shame," Jenna says through a mouthful of melted chocolate and dough. "What?" My sister looks at me as she reaches for her third piece of bacon.

"Nothing," I laugh at her. "I'm really glad we went to visit Dad yesterday. Thank you for doing that, both of you."

I briefly look between my sister and mom. Eating breakfast together—a totally normal experience that feels so right but is still so new to me at the same time. I don't even remember the last time the three of us spent time like this together. It was definitely before Dad died. I try to think back and remember, and surprisingly, it comes to me easily.

"Jenna! Not fair, give it back!" I laughed at my sister as I tried to grab the Monopoly piece from her hand.

"No! I rolled higher, I get to be the dog, fair and square!" she stuck her tongue out at me.

"Now, now, children, do I need to put one of you in time out?" We both laughed at my mom's overly parental voice.

I was sitting on the floor of the living room leaning over the coffee table with my mom, Jenna, and her girlfriend Lacey as we played Monopoly. Friday night game nights were one of my favorite things. They started a while back, when Dad had gone back to work and started staying late at the office for parties or cocktail hours. He never really seemed happy when he came home, but I didn't think much of it because I got to have one of the most fun nights of my life. Jenna would drive over for the night and sometimes bring along her new girlfriend Lacey.

We each took turns picking out the week's game. My favorite was Monopoly because I was always the dog piece. I always wanted a dog, and this was one of the many ways I could hint my desired gift to my mom, hoping she would convince Dad to agree to it. But tonight, Jenna was trying to steal the dog piece from me and I had no idea why.

She was technically right, she did roll higher so she got to pick her piece first. But I didn't understand why she had to pick my piece. The dog was always my piece, she knew that. I was about to make my second choice of the thimble when the doorbell rang.

"Pizza's here!" I screamed and ran to the door with cash in hand. The second best thing about our game night was guaranteed pizza for dinner. Sometimes we changed it up and ordered Chinese instead, but I especially loved pizza nights.

"Don't forget to tip!" my mom yelled as I opened the door.

After it swung inward, I physically took a step back when I saw it wasn't the pizza man, but it was my dad.

"Dad, what are you doing? Why are you ringing the doorbell?" I asked him.

He laughed and rubbed the top of my head with his hand as he walked past me into the house. He was always doing that, even though I was clearly not a little kid anymore. I didn't have the heart to ask him to stop, but would casually fix my hair when I knew he wasn't looking.

"Ben, what's wrong? Did something happen?" my mom asked him, referring to his work, I assumed.

"Oh. everything's fine. They let us go early tonight, that's all."

I remember thinking something was weird about the way he said this, but I was so excited he was there that I didn't care.

"So you can play Monopoly with us!" I grabbed his hand and dragged him over to the coffee table where our game was set up.

"We ordered pizza, it should be here any minute," Jenna said, still holding Lacey's hand.

"Perfect. I'm starving." He winked at me and nodded a brief hello to Jenna's girlfriend. Jenna blushed,

and it made my heart flutter that Dad didn't care who Jenna liked.

"All right, well, you have to roll to be able to pick your piece," my mom said to him, handing him the dice.

"Are you sure you want to play with us?" I asked him. If he got off work early, he could have done anything he wanted.

"Absolutely, kiddo," he ruffled the top of my head again. "There's nothing in this world I would like more."

I glance over at Jenna now, who has returned from serving herself a third round of chocolate chip pancakes. She and my mom are laughing about some crazy plan for asking out her crush in the sorority she's joined. An instinctive feeling takes over, pushing me to both cry and smile at the same time when looking back at them now. I go for the latter and smile at them both, and my heart feels like it's grown three sizes in the span of one weekend.

"Do you guys remember when Dad came home from work early and crashed our Monopoly game?" I ask them.

"Oh, my gosh, yes! I was so nervous sitting there with Lacey, but Dad didn't care. I loved him so much for that moment." Jenna smiles.

We all laugh at the shared memory and it feels so good to be like this. To talk about times when our dad was alive without feeling broken. Sure, we miss him every day and something will always be missing from *us*, but we are so lucky to be here like this, after everything.

We are happy, we are healthy.

We are together.

We may not be perfect and we most definitely have our bruises, but we're healing and finding a way to move on. Together.

And that's good enough for me.

Chapter Fifteen

"I feel like I went through the five stages of grief in the span of forty-eight hours," I laugh and say to Blaze, who is sitting on my bed with me.

After breakfast, I called her and asked her to come by. There's so much I need to say to her, to thank her for. Especially after the other night.

"Isn't that a good thing?" She raises an eyebrow at me.

"I guess, but it still feels weird. Like I don't deserve to feel good or be happy."

"Why don't you deserve that? It's not like it's your fault your dad died." She smiles at me, the sympathy in her eyes overwhelming. My breath catches in my chest at what I have to say next.

I sigh. "But it is."

"What?"

"My dad dying, it's my fault."

It's silent for a few minutes before she takes my hand and starts talking again. "Alex, don't be ridiculous. It was an accident. A really unfortunate, sad accident. But it was completely out of your control."

"But—" I try to say before she cuts me off.

"It's not like you were the one driving the car that hit him. You didn't run that red light, you know that."

I look up at her, tears filling my eyes. "But I might as well have." Honestly, I'm genuinely shocked that my body can even handle generating any more tears after this weekend.

"I don't understand." She expects me to say more.

And so I start talking. I start talking and I don't seem to stop.

I tell her about how after every home game my

dad would stop at Wally's Ice Cream Shop on the way home and get us both our favorite, a double chocolate chip ice cream sandwich, even though she knows this already.

My mouth rambles on about how on the day he died, I had asked to go home with a girl on the team to grab pizza instead of going with him. How I came home later that evening, to find my mom screaming in the doorway and a Wally's Ice Cream Shop receipt sticking out of his wallet that was resting on the kitchen counter. The wallet the police had dropped off in a bag with his other belongings after clearing the scene of the accident.

"No one knows, and no one seemed to really question where my dad was going that day or what he was doing," I gulp back a sob. "But I know. I know exactly where he was going and exactly what he was doing. And it was all because of me."

The breath I release is so deep, it feels like I've been holding it for months.

Because I have.

This is the last thing I'm holding in, the final piece I need to admit to myself. A thousand bricks fall from my shoulders at the words. I've never said them out loud to anyone, not even to my mom or my sister.

No one would understand the meaning behind the receipt in his wallet that day. Only me. And I've been too ashamed to tell anyone else about it. Until now.

Even though I'm still horrified by it, it feels so good to finally tell someone. To admit the greatest mistake of my life.

"Lex, you know that's crazy right?"

I shake my head at her. "No, it's the truth. He's gone and it's all my fault."

"Alex, stop. There is no possible way that his death was your fault. Even with whatever crazy connection to ice cream you're trying to put together."

"But he—"

"No, stop it," she puts her hand up to interrupt me. "I don't care if the man was going to grab a beer or pick up ice cream or head to the movies for that matter. A drunk idiot ran a red light and caused the accident. That crazy person is responsible for taking your dad away, not you. And now he gets to spend the rest of his life in a jail cell, never forgetting what he did. But you—you get to keep going." Her stare is intense and fierce. "You get to live, Alex, and you would be a damn fool not to take advantage of that."

My tear ducts betray me yet again and I start to sob at her words. She brings me into her arms and I feel as though every shudder of breath and tear that escapes is one I've been holding in for far too long.

I'm free, I think. *I'm finally free.*

"If you aren't going to live for yourself," she whispers in my ear. "Then live for him. Live for your dad. He wouldn't want your life spent any other way."

And with her words, I finally realize the truth. She's right. My dad's death wasn't my fault. It was so sudden, so tragic, that I thought I could blame it on someone. Blame it on myself.

But even if I had gone home with him that day, there's no way to know if the accident wouldn't have happened. There's no way to know if I would've died right along with him. The realization of that fact smacks me so hard, I physically have to pull away from Blaze to catch my breath.

"You're right," I smile at her and wipe my face with my sweater. "Thank you."

I squeeze her hand. "God, I don't deserve you. All the shit I've put you through—the popularity, the parties, me falling apart in the front seat of your car. I don't know how you put up with me, but I'm glad you do. Thank you."

Blaze and I sit there for a minute and cry together, until we start laughing about the beginning of the year and my brief rise and fall of popularity.

"Oh, my god, do you remember your skimpy little outfits? And how you roamed around the halls like a lost little puppy without Jordan to follow?" She laughs at me.

The memory makes me flinch. "Gross, don't remind me," I tell her.

It was only a few months ago, but I feel like a completely different person now than I was back then. Part of me wonders what it would be like to go back to that moment when everything felt bright, like I had the whole world at my feet. But then I remember everything that's happened. How no one I knew stood by me while I crashed and burned. No one except for Blaze. She's always here, ready to pick up the pieces when things go bad or throw up her hands in celebration with me when they are good.

No, if I had the chance, I would never go back to the way it was before. I would never want that life back because then who knows what would've happened to me and Blaze. Who knows where I would be now without her. Who I would be.

Jordan might have been my distraction, but Blaze is always going to be my rock.

I stare at her now—she's messing with a button on the side of her ripped black skinny jeans and laughing at another memory she recalled from the start of the school year. I can't help but smile at her and I tell her again how grateful I am to call her my friend.

A saying pops into my mind suddenly. "Grief doesn't get any lighter, but we get used to carrying the weight. If you're lucky enough, you will find people in your life that help you carry it along the way." I think I heard the line on an episode of *Virgin River* my mom was watching a few months ago. At the time, I thought it was cheesy. But now I'm beginning to understand what it means.

I guess I am lucky, in this way. The word makes me think about Cameron and I feel a tug at my heart. He was right about that, too, though not in the way he thought.

I am lucky, but not because my dad died at an age where I can understand his death. I'm lucky to have someone like Blaze in my life who helps me carry this weight, without me even asking her to do it. She never gives up on me, even when I want to give up on myself.

I'm lucky to have my sister and my mom. Two people who will share this tragedy with me for the rest of our lives, but will always be here for me through it.

Maybe this is what life is about, I think. It isn't about the popularity, or the parties, or even the bad things that happen, because bad things will definitely happen. It's about the people you have around you. The ones who will stand by your side and get you through all of it, for better or for worse.

It's about being lucky enough to be loved and to give love in return.

Even Cameron, a boy who I couldn't stand a few weeks ago, has played such a part in my life. My heart flutters at the thought of him, and I know that's going to be a whole other conversation I need to have. Between him, Blaze, and my family, I'm luckier than I know.

I feel like the princess at the end of a fairytale, being swept off her feet by not one but two amazing people in my life. Growing up, I would always wait for the part in the movie where the girl was in trouble, and the guy had to come to rescue her and save the day. I always dreamt of the day someone would love me like that, would come to my rescue if I ever needed it.

Even after my dad died, I think a part of me was waiting for Jordan to save me. To take me away and make everything better.

"Not everything in life is a fairytale movie," Jenna would always say to me.

My sister was right, not everything in life is a fairytale movie. Not every guy is going to save the girl when she's in trouble. Sometimes, more often than we like to admit, the girl has to save herself.

But if she's lucky enough, she won't have to do it alone.

Chapter Sixteen

It's never too late, it's never too late. The words repeat in my head for the thousandth time.

Standing on the dock at Lake Monroe in the chilly November air is probably not the best idea, but I don't want to meet Cam anywhere else. This is our spot.

I haven't talked to him in weeks, not since I stormed away from this very place after he said I was lucky for losing my dad. I wince at the memory, feeling stupid for getting angry with him so quickly without giving him the chance to explain what he meant.

The probability that he's even going to show up today is slim. I'm even surprised he texted me back in the first place. That's if you consider a thumbs up reaction to my **can we talk? I'll be at the lake** text a response, but I'm grasping at straws here.

The sound of his footsteps fill my ears before I can even focus on his figure coming down the pathway. At the sight of him, my whole body tenses up. My heart wants to beat right out of my chest. Will I ever get used to the way I feel when I'm around him?

He looks so good. His hair is a little shorter, tousled perfectly above his forehead. He's wearing dark jeans with a hole near the shin. His black V-neck contrasts against his porcelain skin beautifully, and a leather jacket is draped around his shoulders. The same leather jacket he covered me with in his car the night we first met. My heart instantly pulls at the memory—it feels like that happened a lifetime ago.

He walks toward me slowly with his hands in his front pockets. It takes everything in me not to run over to him and jump into his arms.

I'm suddenly aware of my appearance and how I

probably could have put in a bit more effort for him. Blaze would flip if she saw me right now. I'm in black leggings and a loose teal t-shirt, with a gray bomber jacket that doesn't provide much warmth in the brisk weather. I'm not even in cute booties, I'm wearing my old white Converse. Definitely not a win-the-boy-back outfit. *Ugh.*

He slows down as he approaches me and I watch as his eyes hesitantly move up and down my body. *Great*, I think. I definitely should've thought about my attire before I came here.

"Hi," I say with a small smile.

"Hey," he replies.

We stand there in silence, staring at each other for what feels like hours.

"Listen—" I start.

"So—" he says at the same time.

We both laugh at ourselves and I motion for him to come over to the end of the dock, where we can look out onto the lake. He follows, but keeps his distance. The mere six feet that sits between us feels like thousands of miles instead.

"You go," he says without looking at me. His gaze is focused hard on the outline of the water.

"Okay, um…" I begin. *Damn*, this is harder than I thought it was going to be. I take a breath and decide to go for it. "I guess I should start by saying I'm sorry," I glance over and see his face is still impassive, and I can't tell what he's thinking. "I shouldn't have blown up at you like I did, especially when you were telling me about your mom."

No response. *Keep going, Alex.*

"I don't know if you noticed, but I haven't really been dealing with my dad's death the way I probably should have been," I stifle a small laugh that he doesn't return. *Yikes*, okay. I clear my throat. "After he died, everyone around me kind of moved on with their lives. My mom acted like it never happened, and my sister completely deserted me. It was like we put his body in the ground, wiped the dirt off our hands, and went on to whatever plans we had next."

My hands find the railing of the dock in front of me, my knuckles turning white from how strong I'm holding on.

"It felt so wrong to me, but *everyone* was doing it. I wanted to scream and cry and rip apart the world from the inside out. But no one else was doing that, so it made me feel like I was crazy," I continue. At this, he turns his body to face me and the look on his face seems to change from anger to understanding. At least, I hope that's what I'm seeing.

"You're not crazy."

He stares at me and for a moment I get lost in the ocean blue hues of his eyes. "I felt the same way, in a way," he starts to say. "Not after my mom died, but before. My dad did everything he could to prevent her death. Of course, he's no doctor, but he would never talk about the details of it. He would act like she was in the hospital for a checkup, and not stage-4 cancer. I wasn't stupid, but I was young. I didn't know what to question and what to go along with."

I reach for his hand and he doesn't pull away. "I'm so sorry."

My body reacts to the touch immediately, a blast of heat and electricity running up my arm. He quickly looks down at where our hands meet, and for a moment I wonder if he can feel it, too. And if he's felt it this entire time we've been around each other.

"It's fine," he shrugs. "Not much I can do about it now."

"I don't get it," I laugh lightly and shake my head. "How are we supposed to say goodbye to someone who has been such a huge part of our lives, if no one even acknowledges that they're gone?"

He stares at me with a small smile and my breath catches in my throat.

"I don't know." He takes my hand and starts to intertwine our fingers together. I feel my cheeks blush. "But I don't think we need to say goodbye. I think we need to carry them with us every day, and know that in some way, they're always around."

All I can do is offer him a small nod, his words making my eyes water.

"I didn't mean you were lucky that your dad died, and I hate that that must be what you think of me," he adds. I tighten my grip in his hand, and look back at him.

"I know, and I don't think that. I was mad at first, but I don't think I was mad at what you said. I think I was mad because part of me knew you were calling me out for avoiding my grief, but I wasn't ready to accept that," I start to explain. "I think in a way, I didn't want to believe that I needed to grieve. Because acknowledging that meant acknowledging my dad was really gone."

He nods in a way that tells me he gets it. And he really does, I think. He gets it more than anyone else I know.

I tell him about my breakdown with Blaze, and how that prompted a well overdue conversation with my mom and my sister.

"What made you snap?" he asks me, and I can tell he's genuinely curious.

"Jordan did," I say and notice how his body tenses at the mention of his name and he scoffs under his breath. *Is he jealous?*

"He and I talked at Bev's party and he wanted to

get back together."

Cameron's eyes leave mine and stare back out at the water. He nods his head once again, as if he understands what happened. But I would bet money he doesn't.

"The whole interaction with him made me realize that Paige was right," I say and briefly explain what Paige said to me. "I don't think I was ever with Jordan for the right reasons. I hate admitting that, the kind of person that makes me sound like, but it's the truth."

"And now?" he asks, still keeping his gaze across the lake. I want to put my hand on his cheek and bring his eyes back to mine.

"I don't want to be with someone for my own selfish reasons. I don't want to be that kind of girl anymore. The next person I'm with, I want it to be real."

He tilts his head to the right, looking as though he's thinking my words over. His lips purse slightly, and I get the feeling he feels the same way. I only hope he feels that way about me.

"So what happened with your family?" he asks.

I tell him about visiting my dad's grave, and he starts rubbing the back of my hand with his fingers that aren't holding my own. Totally unaware of the trail of heat he's leaving behind with every stroke.

I mention how I told my sister I believe our dad will always be with us, always watching over us from wherever he is now. He smiles lightly at that. His Adam's apple bobs and I can tell he's trying not to shed a tear. The vulnerability of this moment hits me as fast as the fresh breeze that blows over us, the chill temperature sending a shiver through my body.

"I feel my mom in the wind," he says and I look over to see his eyes are closed, he's breathing deeply through the breeze. "I see her in my eyes and I hear her in my little brother's laugh. Those small moments keep me going. The ones where I can sense she's still with me."

I never thought about that, finding ways to recognize the person you miss the most in the spaces and people all around you. The ways they are still here.

"My sister has his smile," I say and can't help the grin that takes over my face. "And I can still hear his excited screams when I score a goal during a soccer game. I feel him here, at the lake—he always loved being on the water." I smile as the thoughts leave my mouth. Here Cameron goes again, pushing me to think about things in an entirely different way.

"See? He's not gone, not completely. He's still with you, and if you let yourself see that, you'll always find him."

I smile at him. "Because I'm lucky, in that way."

His grin smirks to the side of his mouth and I fight the urge to kiss him right then and there. Instead, I look out to the water and watch the colors of the sky change from pink to purple as the sun starts to set.

Sitting here, holding Cameron's hand, I finally feel like everything is going to be okay. Like *I'm* going to be okay.

"Thank you," I say to him.

"For what?"

"For everything," I roll my eyes. "I don't know how much longer I could've gone on like I was. You pushed me to see the truth, to take off the mask and face the music, so to speak. It sucked, believe me. But I needed it."

He shrugs and looks over to me, our faces so close together that if either one of us tilts our heads at the right angle…

"I saw something in you that I saw in myself and I thought you could use a friend." His sentence interrupts my thoughts and I freeze in place at the word. *A friend?* I hate that word, hate how it sounds coming out of his mouth. That's the last thing I want him to be, my *friend*.

I want so much more.

The surge of confidence I've felt all weekend resurfaces and I think *this is my chance*. I should tell him how I feel. *Here goes nothing, Alex*. The honesty train isn't going to stop here.

"I don't know if I can be your friend. *Just* your friend." I smile shyly, but can't break my gaze from his eyes. Those eyes... the swirling waves of blues and greens and golds. I can easily get lost in them forever.

Being around him feels so right, like this is exactly where I'm supposed to be. Every time he touches me, my skin burns with desire and my entire body aches when he pulls away. What I feel for Cameron is more than what someone would feel for a friend. And I think he knows that.

His eyes are still staring into mine and for a moment I feel like he can see right through me, straight into my entire soul. He can have it. He can have all of it, for all I care.

His gaze drifts briefly down to my lips and back up to my eyes so fast, I would've missed it if I blinked. I bite my lip in response.

"I told you to stop doing—" I start to say but am interrupted because his mouth is on mine before I can finish.

Both of his hands are on the sides of my face and he kisses me gently, so soft and quick that before I know it I'm staring back into his eyes again and he's looking at me desperately, asking a question without even forming any words. A second later, he does.

"Are you sure?" he asks me, looking between my eyes and my lips once more. His question makes me smile and I run my fingers through his hair. I watch as his eyes flutter closed, then open again. Those gorgeous blue and emerald flaked eyes, the tragedy in them so clear, a perfect reflection to my own pair. But now there's something else there, too—something brighter and shinier.

Like a glimmer of hope.

I smile at him and quickly nod my head. As his lips brush mine, I feel something inside my chest unlock. Something I haven't felt in a really long time.

We break apart briefly before crashing back into each other with a new sense of urgency, and I'm suddenly reminded of the lecture in Mr. Salts' class about mitosis. I can't believe I'm thinking about biology right now, but I can't help but wonder if my teacher knew how real that lesson was for me, even if I didn't know it myself at the time.

Mitosis isn't just a term found in a biology textbook.

It's a definition for life.

Because in life, there are going to be times when we fall down. There are going to be moments when we break apart, when we feel so low we can't possibly see a way out. But sometimes cells are meant to break apart, if only so they can find their way back together again.

Forming a new version of themselves, over and over.

The End

ACKNOWLEDGEMENTS

A huge thanks to Stacey Adderley at Evernight Teen for taking a chance on this story. I received the email offering to publish LUCKY ENOUGH on the anniversary of my father's death, and I immediately knew it was meant to be. I can't thank Stacey enough for all her kind words and assistance throughout this process.

A major shoutout to my inner circle of the Writing Community and all the critique partners, beta readers, and new friends I have made in this world. Thank you all for providing such strong input and feedback as I wrote this story, and ultimately helping me make it the best it can be. Thank you to Isabelle and Jessica, for prompting me to go in a different direction and allowing me to love every minute of it.

To my husband, thank you for being my biggest fan and a huge influence for Cameron's character. Your love and support for my passions and dreams of writing has filled me with so much joy, and I hope a piece of our love story can pay tribute to that here.

Finally, to my dad, who I miss more each and every day. This one's for you, and I know you are looking down on me now and smiling proudly. I'll carry you with me forever.

ANDIE L. SMITH

LUCKY ENOUGH

ANDIE L. SMITH

Evernight Teen ®

<u>**www.evernightteen.com**</u>